"In the valley the gun crews and the tank crews stood silently by their smoking weapons . . ."

On the left-hand slopes of the hill the platoons of Dog Company progressed, creeping through the bracken towards the summit, storming the weapon-pits which still resisted.

The first platoon of Dog mounted to the summit on the east side, and encountered fresh resistance from enemy dug in on the reverse slopes. There raged on the knife-edged crest of a hill a desperate struggle for supremacy.

Mason injected fresh enthusiasm into the flagging will of the platoons in the center, urging them forward with a furious example, singling out each foxhole for a hail of rifle-fire before eventually they were near enough to drop a grenade in upon the occupants who cowered inside.

Parkington's platoon, with a final rush, gained the summit on the western edge and joined in the melee which raged for possession.

The Chinese occupying the foxholes on the reverse side leaped out and ran as the whole crest of the hill swarmed with men; as they fled for the valley they were shot down like deer into the shrubbery.

It was four hours since the assault companies had crossed the start-line.

Hill 327 was won.

NOW THRIVE THE ARMOURERS

*A Story of Action with the
Gloucesters in Korea
(November 1950 – April 1951)*

ROBERT O. HOLLES

BANTAM BOOKS
NEW YORK · TORONTO · LONDON · SYDNEY · AUCKLAND

NOW THRIVE THE ARMOURERS

A Bantam Book / published by arrangement with the author

PRINTING HISTORY
First published in Great Britain in 1952
Bantam edition / November 1989

Drawings by Greg Beecham.
Maps by Alan McKnight.

ISBN 0-553-28321-9

Published simultaneously in the United States and Canada

PRINTED IN THE UNITED STATES OF AMERICA

OPM   0 9 8 7 6 5 4 3 2 1

To
E.E.H.

Now all the youth of England are on fire,
And silken dalliance in the wardrobe lies:
Now thrive the armourers, and honour's thought
Reigns solely in the breast of every man.

Henry V, Act II, Prologue

CONTENTS

PREFACE

In the pages which follow I have attempted to trace and portray the activities of the 1st Battalion of the Gloucestershire Regiment during the retreat from Pyongyang and the subsequent events leading up to the battle of Solma-ri—the Imjin battle.

Due to the confused circumstances which still remain, more than a year after the conclusion of that action, the fate of a number of the British casualties is still obscure, and to avoid possible embarrassment to the relatives of those killed and missing I have used fictitious names.

The characters who revolve around Parkington's platoon, through whom the story is unfolded, are drawn from my own store of impressions as typical of those men who first set foot in Korea with great reluctance, and ended by winning imperishable honour for their regiment.

The incidents and the general narrative are based upon reality, and for some aspects of the battle of Solma-ri I am indebted to surviving members of the battalion. Of the battle of Solma-ri itself, the final chapter—that of the fate of the majority, who struck south in their attempt at a break-out—remains to be written when the prisoners-of-war in Chinese hands are released.

R. O. H.

I

ARRIVAL

As the great white bulk of the trooper *Empire Windrush* edged a passage through a shoal of sleek U.S. Navy destroyers anchored in Pusan harbour the sergeant-major assembled his company below decks. He was a portly Irishman: he spoke with a thick brogue, shifting his ponderous weight continually from one foot to the other. His speech was brief and impressive.

U.S. Navy Destroyer

"Ye've finished wi lazin' about on the decks, so ye have. Don't none of ye's be thinkin' the War's over, for it is not. An' even if it is there's no time to be slackin' off. Oi'll have me eyes on every one of ye's, wherever ye might be. An' if ye start to hear the bullets singin' past ye there's no use in startin' to run, for if ye're meant for a bullet ye'll get it just the same, an' ye won't hear it comin'. Now, get away an' finish ye're packin' up, for when it's toime to go ashore Oi don't want to find any one of ye's missin'. Dismiss!"

As the company broke up Hurst said, "Cheerful, ain't 'e? Proper laughin' boy, 'im."

Corporal Woodbridge murmured, "Must say I don't go much on the fatalistic attitude."

"An' stop the talkin'," shouted the sergeant-major over their retreating backs.

There had been, in fact, little time for swanning under tropical skies during the trip. Each day was devoted to rigid training. The decks had been alive with little cadres of men taking lectures, practising arms-drill and physical training. The whole ship vibrating to the rattle of firearms, firing into the water from the stern. . . .

There had been no day of rest from the Bay of Biscay to the China Sea.

The quay was hung with a vast banner shouting the legend WELCOME, UNITED NATIONS FORCES, surrounded by a galaxy of their flags, dominated by the Union Jack, and flanked by the Stars and Stripes, the Dove of the United Nations, and the incongruous sphere and bars of the South Korean Republic. The flags fluttered and dipped in a strong breeze, flaunting their colours against the background of dull sky: just such a sky might be gathering over Epping Forest on the same November day.

While the ship berthed a reception committee appeared on the quay as magically as a pantomime chorus. Korean girls dressed in dazzling silk kimonos waved minute Union Jacks with mechanical industry. The sound of rattles brought forth the response of a thin, inarticulate cheer from the crowded upper decks. The ranks of kimonos parted to receive a small group of Korean officials, who shouldered their way to the front with the assurance of V.I.P.'s, and waited deferentially with the obsequious air of the Oriental.

Bursting upon this Gilbertian parade, a U.S. military band composed entirely of Negroes blared a daring version of *Colonel Bogey* at twice its natural tempo. A huge grinning drum-major performed the ritual of a witch-doctor in front. The band marched and counter-marched along the whole length of the quay, under a long frontage of grey warehouses.

The ship's captain and the Battalion Commander disembarked to be officially welcomed by a dapper major of the U.S. Army. They were introduced to a Korean officer resplendent in gold braid, and the leading citizen came forward awkwardly, to be presented. He was dressed in a dark pinstripe suit which sagged in the hollows of his frame; a respectable black Homburg overshadowed the features of a vulture. He carried a rolled umbrella. Two dusky little girls were pushed forward to present a bouquet of chrysanthemums to the colonel. A full-throated cheer rose from the starboard decks. The leading

citizen dropped his umbrella. The band raced through
St. Louis Blues, with obvious relish. The colonel
brandished the bouquet overhead. He appeared faintly
embarrassed. The leading citizen retrieved his umbrella and proceeded to dust it with a gaudy handkerchief. A mournful howl from the ship's siren. . . .

It was on November 9, 1950, that the 1st Battalion of the Gloucestershire Regiment landed in Korea,
with other units of the 29th Brigade. They were
composed chiefly of reservists who had been disturbed, rudely, from their civilian way of life, to
combat the new Communist menace in the East. The
bulk of the battalion's officers and N.C.O.'s were
regulars. There was a sprinkling of National Service
volunteers.

All walks of life were represented in this polyglot company, sharing, at first, only the common
yearning to "get back to Blighty," and the common
resentment at having to "come all this bloody way to
mind somebody else's business." It was not their war.
Men who wore a gallery of ribbons won in hot battle
during the Second World War were not disposed
kindly towards fighting an obscure campaign in a
country they had never heard of for a cause which
had so many ramifications which they could not quite
grasp.

But by November the North Korean armies had
been shattered and broken and hurled back to the
Yalu river, on the Manchurian border. There would
possibly be a bit of mopping-up to be done. That was
all. It was nearly all over. Soon they would be home,

ARRIVAL 5

carrying on with the business of living. All the same, it was a "bloody nuisance."

In a union of the worst elements in each, East and West meet in the foul cosmopolitan slum which is Pusan. Behind the great sheds and warehouses and giant derricks of the dock area lie the acres of goods marshalling-yards and stores depots which have mushroomed to their purpose in the midst of the squalor of the native quarters. Among the flimsy wooden shacks which seem to huddle together like old widowed sisters for mutual support the atmosphere is as pregnant with filth and corruption as the narrow streets are foul with the reek of rotting garbage.

A persistent drizzle of rain pattered on the corrugated iron roof of the sheds which serve Pusan for a station building as the battalion entrained. The small engine seemed quite inadequate to cope with the long line of wagons, the mounds of baggage on the platforms waiting to be loaded on. Inside the wagons were equipped with hard wooden seats. Each was soon filled to capacity with men, blankets, kitbags, boxes, rifles, ration-crates, and cookhouse equipment. There was an interminable wait before the engine uttered a long-drawn-out wail, and the carriages began slowly to move in a series of bone-jarring jerks. It was not a pleasant journey.

The distance of some two hundred miles to Suwon occupied three days. The space was so restricted that it was impossible to ease the limbs. At night the darkness was absolute, and it was bitterly cold. Icy draughts penetrated the vacant windows, weaving a cross-current of discomfort through the carriage.

Sleep was virtually impossible. The men sprawled under their blankets in any position likely to afford rest. During the day the sun shone synthetically, without heat, lighting the changeless panorama of terraced rice-fields stretching chessboard-like to the lower slopes of gaunt hills.

The catastrophe of war had visited this land, and before departing had seared its brand so deeply as to obscure the image of what had once been. It seemed that the landscape which slowly traversed the windows of the train was ravaged by nature, rather than war—a timeless devastation.

On the fringes of the winding, dust-covered roads the noses of burnt-out tanks protruded like lizards, and the black and brown of their gaunt bodies was the black and brown of the rice-fields, of the hills. Bomb-craters which dimpled the riverbeds under ruined bridges were as familiar to their surroundings as craters on the surface of the moon. The complexities of the rusting undersides of an overturned lorry blended into the dismal wreckage of masonry and rubble where a row of dwellings had once stood. Occasionally, where the railway had been blasted, a line of shattered wagons, a ghost train riddled and twisted and gutted by fire, would stand in a siding surrounded by a mass of blasted rails, like decaying serpents from the severed head of a Gorgon.

Objects such as these were no longer transitional traffic. They had achieved a degree of permanency which made them an integral part, almost necessarily component to their surroundings.

The train, with maddening perversity, stopped often, and for no apparent reason. At each small

station platform the train was surrounded by hordes
of ragged children and emaciated old women, beg-
ging for food, fighting each other to collect the scraps
of biscuits and chocolate which were showered from
the carriage windows.

Food was prepared on the platform or beside
the rails when the train stopped long enough for the
purpose. The cooks produced hash with a medley of
corned beef, dehydrated potato, and crushed Army
biscuit. It was not calculated to satisfy a sensitive
palate. Repetition made it a dull offering. . . .

Hurst, the driver, surveying the glutinous mass
in his mess-tin, said gloomily, "Worst since I was in
the nick, this. If my missus shoved this lot under my
nose I'd sling it out the window. No messin'." He
spat out a mouthful of tea. "An' this after it!"

"What about the old woman?" prompted Lane
from the opposite seat.

"She'd go first." In reality, Hurst's wife was a
tiny, vociferous woman whose cooking was above
reproach.

Eventually the train had drawn slowly into Suwon
station, and was vomiting forth its human cargo. Rain
had begun to fall again. It was billowing through the
broken roof of the soot-ingrained station building,
and fine raindrops clung like tiny sequins to the
battledress of the men who now swarmed over the
station area. The platform overflowed into a disused
goods yard which had become a quagmire of oozing
yellow slime, lacerated with huge ruts.

Confusion attended the next hour, as the battalion detrained, a confusion of vague forms struggling in the early-morning half-light.

Kit was piled up in the yard and stowed aboard U.S. Army lorries with grinning Negro drivers, which roared off, almost immediately running into top gear. The men standing on the platform had resolved themselves into shivering groups hastily organizing wood fires. A handful of Korean railway-workers gaped vacuously. At irregular and frequent intervals the piercing note of a train-whistle sounded through the station.

In the area behind the goods yard, where Hurst and Lane went in search of wood, the ground was littered with debris. Every piece of combustible material had been gathered long since. There was no sign of human habitation, apart from a single small shack. They confronted it. Lane studied the structure intently.

"That door looks a bit flimsy. 'E might come orf."

The door was indeed frail. It yielded easily to a concerted pull from outside, with a loud splintering of rotten wood. Inside the hut they could dimly discern a number of prostrate figures on camp-beds. A voice shouted, "Say, what the hell——" It had a strong American accent.

"Sorry, mate," Hurst called out cheerfully. They carried the door back to the station platform, where they discovered, pinned to the inside of the door, a printed card which bore the simple legend "Home, Sweet Home."

They removed it before the door was broken up and consigned to the flames.

*   *   *

Finally each company mustered its platoons, and the battalion began to march to its destination, a long ribbon of khaki against the dirt-caked surface of the narrow road which led away from the station.

Weighed down with kit as they were, the pace was a slow shamble. Lane's bulging pack chafed his shoulders, and his rifle slid down until it swung freely from his elbow.

Sloan, the platoon sergeant, shouted continuously, "Keep in step at the rear! Close up! Lane, you look like you've been on the batter for a month! Keep up, man!"

It seemed an age before the front of the column wheeled into a courtyard beyond which reared the impressive façade of Suwon University. Behind the imposing lines of the architecture there was the prospect of wide, draughty rooms with broken windows, open, wind-swept corridors, and the accumulation of garbage which had accrued from six months of occupation and evacuation by troops moving towards the battlefront.

It had been a tiring day in a succession of days of tiredness. Lane, fond of sleep, climbed underneath his blankets directly it was convenient to do so. Hurst disappeared on a night operation of his own. Corporal Woodbridge, groping about in a musty locker-room full of Japanese text-books, had chanced to find a batch of 1932 copies of the *Farmer and Stock-breeder*. He pored over them, after dark, by the guttering light of a candle. Somebody in the room was brewing-up tea on a paraffin stove which smoked alarmingly. The C.Q.M.S. brought round the rum ration. Sergeant Sloan, inwardly cursing his ill-luck, was mounting the night guard. The battalion was settling in. . . .

II

GUERRILLA WARFARE

At ten the next morning the Brigade Commander turned up to address all officers and N.C.O.'s of the battalion. They were accommodated in a draughty lecture-room. The brigadier spoke of the need for caution in estimating the enemy resources. He mentioned the possibility of Chinese intervention. And he outlined the reasons for the whole affair for the benefit of the skeptically-minded.

But Parkington—Lieutenant Charles Parkington—was fresh from Sandhurst and in no mood to probe too deeply into the reasons for his presence in that audience. It was enough that he had arrived in this, his first campaign, to be blooded for a career in which his roots were already deep. None of the traditional and frustrating years of futile training; this was to be warfare in real earnest, unless the other people packed in. He secretly hoped that they wouldn't; not yet. The ideology of the thing was not important.

But the sentiments of Corporal Woodbridge were closely related to the brigadier's words. A conscript himself, he had been reading law until the call-up

11

notice had slipped into his correspondence to change the sphere of his activities.

Avoiding the irritations of O.C.T.U.'s, he had volunteered for Korea, where he proposed to study the situation at close hand.

The sergeant-major, standing near the door, was listening attentively. There was a distant hammering from the farther end of the building. He was debating whether to send a corporal to have it stopped.

Sergeant Sloan hardly listened at all. He was an old soldier, seventeen years' service, and had once been a sergeant-major himself, until a brief clash with authority had occasioned him to start all over again. Hot climates had bleached his thinning hair. He was bitter and disillusioned. He had seen wars before, and this one, if it persisted, was going to be a more squalid and uncomfortable business than anything in his experience. Sloan detested the idea of continuous hard living. Perhaps, later on, there would be a chance of a medical board. . . .

Lieutenant Gilmour, who commanded the next platoon in Parkington's company, said, "Well, Charlie-boy, now you know all the griff. Nothing a close secret any more." Gilmour was a hearty, bluff sort of fellow, a school-teacher in civilian life, called up on reserve. He was no longer very young. Parkington half liked, half resented his over-genial approach.

"Know something else, Charlie? There's a big O-group at Baker-How-Queen in half an hour."

Parkington said, "What's it all about?"

"Nothing definite yet. I think there's a scheme

coming off. Battalion in attack; getting acclimatized; you know the sort of thing."

"My God, Mike, haven't we come out here to do the thing in earnest?"

"I wish I could answer that question for you, Charlie-boy," Gilmour said absently. "Like to have one of my American cigarettes—Chesterfields?"

The companies set out at dawn, three days later, marching to a destination in the hills, seven miles away. For Mr Parkington's platoon, detailed to defend the right flank of the company positions, it was a bad day.

Hurst complained bitterly at being included as an extra rifleman on a scheme. The battalion transports had been delayed at sea, and had not yet arrived in the country.

The platoon was detailed to dig positions in a rice-field which commanded a river-crossing, although, as Powell, the signaller, said, "T'ain't no use; b-blewdy river's dried up, any'ow, so any f-fool could er-git acrorst if they wanted to." Water gurgled through the soft clay at the bottom of the foxholes, filling them waist-deep. The Bren-gunners had forgotten to bring their spare barrels. Parkington hoped nobody would notice this. The rest of the company were out of sight, on a hill-top a mile away.

Time dragged on. Parkington consulted his watch every few minutes. He began to look worried. "They should have been here," he confided to Sergeant Sloan, "long before this. Where on earth is Captain Mason?"

Twenty minutes later Captain Mason appeared along the river-bed, waving a map-case.

"'E's doin' 'is tank," said Hurst, with great satisfaction. "It's an absolute balls-up, if you ask me."

"What are you doing here, Mr. Parkington? Waiting for reinforcements? You should have received my signal to move to point Roger an hour ago."

"No signals received, sir," Parkington shouted in reply.

"Well, get cracking now. You're supporting the company flank in the attack on hill two-eight-o. We can't start till you get up, so you'll have to move like hell."

"Very good, sir."

The platoon moved forward at a shambling trot.

The wind had strengthened now, and the light rain which had marred their activities in the morning had now turned to stinging sleet. Parkington's platoon took up positions behind a slight rise which concealed them from the defenders of Hill 280. Only the Bristolian, Lane, kept up any pretence of cheerfulness; Corporal Woodbridge laboured under the strain of a great weariness; Hurst swore perpetually in short bursts of loquacious energy. Sergeant Sloan, back from a reconnaissance, reported that the assault was under way.

"Lay down smoke, three-fifty, straight ahead."

Allen, the mortarman, had been aching for a chance to use what the rest of the platoon cynically called "the drainpipe." In a flurry of activity, conscious of the awe inspired, the 2-inch mortar was mounted, sighted, and a business-like bomb was slid

Russian T 34

into the muzzle. Allen's boots slithered on the wet ground as he pressed against the firing-lever, and the bomb whistled past his head, soaring vertically. The platoon went to ground with remarkable efficiency. Only Allen stayed, staring after the projectile. It was absent for several agonizing seconds.

"Here she comes; watch your heads!" The bomb came to earth, solidly, thirty yards away. Wreaths of smoke curled from it and enveloped the platoon in a white fog.

The subsequent attack was easily repulsed by the defenders. As night fell the battalion reassembled and began the long march back to Suwon.

Several days later every one was preparing for the move to Sibyon-ni.

At this stage of the war in Korea the guerrilla menace was at its peak. The American and South Korean armies, having regained the initiative from the Communists, had pushed forward their tank and infantry columns along the roads to the north, taking town after town, which yielded only a handful of prisoners, while their aircraft constantly harried the retreating enemy to the borders of Manchuria. But the swift advance had cut off and by-passed large groups of North Koreans who had retreated into the hills, and continued to operate as a fighting force by sudden ambuscades, by sniping at vehicles on the supply routes, and by occasional raids in force upon small military formations. They were equipped, still, with Russian arms and ammunition. Many of them lived openly in the villages of the north, operating at night. It was the first operation of the 29th Brigade, which included the Royal Ulster Rifles and the Royal Northumberland Fusiliers, with the tanks of the 8th Hussars, and supporting troops, to hunt down the strong guerrilla forces which roamed the mountains area nort of Kaesong, just across the 38th Parallel.

There was a valley, bordered on three sides by barren hills, and running down on the west side to a plain where a stream trickled down into the village of Sibyon-ni. The village was a desolation of ruined huts standing among acres of debris. A Russian T34 tank rested near the stream with its gun ludicrously twisted upward; like a silent testimonial.

The valley itself was desolate. The lower slopes were pimpled with the circular burial-mounds of a Korean cemetery; many of them were built of fresh soil. Thin lines of stunted firs struggled down from the hill-tops, which were covered with coarse brown scrub. There was no life in the valley; no birds sang. The hills, dappled like the wing of a partridge, stretched beyond the horizons on all sides.

Somewhere among the hills were seven thousand guerrillas.

Here, among the graves, the battalion arrived on the 24th of November, and commenced to dig itself in.

In the morning, at six o'clock, the sun rose, pearl-tinting the eastern hills. At this time the cold was most insistent. The first rays of the sun pierced the thin air like swords of ice.

The hills began to appear in silhouette through a faint white haze, purpling into the far distance, and the intense cold seemed to fill the whole empty void of the universe like a tangible reality. The frost in the valley was like a light fall of snow, so heavily did it lie. But even before first light there was a stirring among the weapon-pits and dugouts which had been hewn from the rock-hard surface of the ground, and the voices of retiring sentries shouting "Stand-to."

The weapon-pits were suddenly peopled by grey forms. There was always bitter comment. . . .

"Whassa time? Can't be time for stand-to already. On'y just got in kip."

"Take yer foot aht o' me ear, can't yer?"

"Oh, —— your ear. It's ——ing cold. Where's me ——ing rifle?"

"Come on, Mike. Time to stand-to."

"Oh-aaah! Who'd be a soldier? What's the time?"

"Half-five. Hurry up and get dressed."

"No tea this morning?"

"Later. No fires until after stand-to. Remember?"

"Hell! I say, Charlie-boy, isn't it bloody cold?"

During the day patrols filed out into the hills, or roared through the village in carriers. Information

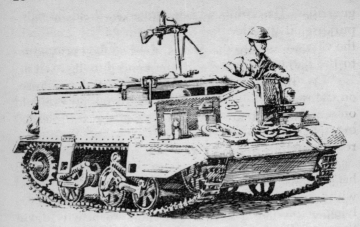

Universal Carrier

filtered through from Korean agents posted in the surrounding villages. The battery of artillery which was leaguered in the centre of the valley occasionally sent a salvo of 25-pounder shells into a distant and obscure target. The transport arrived in a long column from Kaesong. The hills pulsated to the roar of engines.

An old man was brought in for interrogation. His head was covered in coarse, matted hair; in his ragged, filthy clothing he resembled some fanatical anchorite from an earlier century.

A strong carrier force from Support Company was sent to a village where guerrillas were suspected to be building a stronghold. Closing in at dawn, they found a hundred men and a small arsenal. An interpreter was sent for, and the Koreans were questioned.

It was a mistake, they said. They were policemen, formed to protect the village from attack by guerrillas. The arms had been given to them for this purpose. It was decided to let them go. By nightfall the village was abandoned. One of the carriers returning to the battalion lines was disabled by a mine.

On the following day a platoon of C Company, on the way to search another village, were ambushed on a narrow track. As the first fusillade of shots rang out the men instinctively took cover, and began to return the fire.

It was a short engagement. The first onslaught had killed two, injured eight. When the Communists withdrew they left a dozen of their number, lifeless, lying among the trees which concealed them from the road. Reinforcements were called up to scour the area, but the guerrillas had vanished into the hills. First blood had been drawn.

Parkington was relaxing inside his bivouac when Gilmour came in, looking tired and jaded from the day's patrol-work. "Got a bit of news," he said. "Just been given out by the Adj. The Chinks have joined in."

Parkington sat up, suddenly alert. "Really?" he said. "All of 'em?"

"No. Only about half a million. They haven't called on their front-line reinforcements yet. These are just volunteers, violently opposed to capitalists like you and me."

Removing his boots, Parkington said, "I rather hoped something like this would happen. Looks as if we're really going to have a scrap after all."

"Before this business is over you'll probably wish we had nothing to do with it. There's a lot of

Chinese, and a lot of good men will go west before this is over. If you think it's going to be a picnic you'd better think again."

Gilmour disappeared into the outer darkness. Parkington stared after him in surprise.

III

ADVANCE—AND RETREAT

The urgent order to leave Sibyon-ni came at 8
A.M. There remained two hours to dismount the
guns, load the trucks and carriers, and move out. . . .

The settlement of bivouacs remained intact; elab-
orate dwellings, some of them carefully fashioned out
of corrugated iron, wooden stakes, and slats of timber, by the hands of men experienced in this sort of
architecture. Hastily constructed signs outside platoon and company headquarters were left standing
after the inmates had gone. Breakfast, shaving, brewing-
up, and all other activities were abandoned in the
surge of activity which followed the announcement.
It was a prelude to a series of similar sudden moves
which were to occur in the following two months,
when a sudden order to pack up could be expected at
any time of the day or night. It was a nerve-racking
experience. No one was ever sure what was likely to
happen next.

The move from Sibyon-ni was accomplished in
time. The lorries, packed to their canopies, roared
away in a long convoy through the dead village, past
the gorge where a dead guerrilla sprawled at the

bottom of a rock-face, a prominent figure dressed in traditional white, with the face, blackened by frost, staring upward at the straggling trees. Heading north, the convoy started on the long journey to the northern capital of Pyongyang.

Fresh lines of transport arrived in the valley to convey the battalion to the station at Kaesong.

The railway again. . . . Kaesong station was a drab replica of the other stations of the line of towns— Pusan, Taegu, Taejon, Chonan, Suwon, Seoul—which stretch along the backbone of Korea, milestones of progress in many grim battles, which had fallen, devastated, behind the tide of battle, and were devastated again when the tide rolled back.

A long line of cattle-wagons stood ready to continue the journey to the north. Most of them appeared to have been sprayed with machine-gun bullets; the roofs and walls were full of holes; a number of them were without doors.

"I remember seeing something like this in *Punch* once," Gilmour reflected. "It was funny, at the time."

Hurst, driving one of the heavy three-tonners, felt drowsy and comfortable, shut out of the cold, with the engine radiating heat throughout the driving-cab, but he had been driving for six hours, he had had no sleep on the previous night, and his eyelids were beginning to droop. The road continued endlessly, curving and twisting in its baffling route. It was unsurfaced, and continual traffic had worn huge ruts and pot-holes in it. He was forced to use all his concentration. It was a dark night. The glare of approaching headlights dazzled him. Once a convoy of U.S. lorries throttled past at a dangerous speed, one of them swinging and boring him into the side, causing him to brake hard, and earning a volley of abuse from his vitriolic tongue.

Following the lorry in front, Hurst drove on through the night over the worst road he had ever known. By midnight he was desperately tired, and his eyes ached with their constant vigil. Many times he had rearranged his cramped limbs in the restricted space of the cab, but there was no relief from the nagging strain on his overtaxed body. The desire to sleep was almost overpowering. By a conscious effort of will he forced his brain to react against the stupor which fought for the possession of his mental faculties.

He went through all the driver's daily tasks in his mind, and found that he had forgotten two. Recalling them occupied half an hour. Old, half-remembered incidents in his former Army life flickered through his mind like slides on the screen at a lantern lecture—as the day, in Italy, he found a deserted wine-cellar in the ruins of a villa at Rimini. He and his mates had got well and truly sozzled, and finished up by rolling a barrel back to the billets. . . . And, coming back to Naples in the C.O.'s Humber, he had knocked over a young priest who turned out to be wearing a Wehrmacht uniform and major's insignia under his clerical garb. . . . They had shoved him in the nick for borrowing the Humber, just the same. . . . And the girl at the place near Brussels, just like a film star in looks, and wanted to marry him after the War. . . . What a night it was when the War was over. . . . Nothing in this war like the last one—

all bleeding go, no mistake about that. . . . Two years in civvy street, docking, Union rates, very nice, thank you, and now they have to go and pull his number out of the hat and send him out to this hell-hole. "I'm so tired," he thought, "so damn' tired," his head swaying over the steering-wheel.

"I must keep thinking," his conscience thundered; "must think of something else . . . anything. . . ."

The leading truck pulled into a vacant field at the roadside, and the convoy were signalled to park. Soon after Hurst had switched off his engine a sergeant shouted through the door of the cab, "O.K. We move again at o-six hundred hours. Got it?" Hurst was asleep over the wheel at which he had spent the last thirteen hours.

The hard frosts of the preceding nights had prepared the ground for the fresh carpet of snow which fell during the day that the battalion arrived at Pyongyang station and were rushed up in lorries to take up positions among a line of pine-forested hills a few miles to the north of the city, close to the main supply route to the north. The familiar task of digging trenches and building bivouacs began at once.

Dusk fell before the battalion had settled in. There was no moon; only the eerie translucence of the snow cast a faint glow over the area.

Parkington and Sergeant Sloan dug together, muffled against the cold in their overcoats, breathing stertorously, exchanging few words.

Hurst and Lane worked on their communal trench,

stopping only to exchange curses about the weather, the military hierarchy, conditions as a whole. Woodbridge dug in silence, feeling the frost creep into his feet, despite his exertions, and the strain on his muscles, which had never been attuned to hard physical excesses.

Eventually, well into the night, the Company Commander, inspecting the platoon lines with Parkington, deemed the defences to be satisfactory and drew Parkington aside.

"To put you in the picture," he said, "we are doing a rearguard this time. The whole line is pulling back through Pyongyang, and the brigade has been moved up here to see that everybody gets away safely. We don't know where the Chinese are, but they're moving up pretty quickly, and they ought to be here in a day or two. Listen!"

Standing motionless, Parkington could hear, above the sighing of pines, the continuous throb of engines from the main supply route, which lay over a low ridge to the east.

"You'll hear plenty of that in the near future. There are two American Divisions coming through here, as well as the 27th Brigade, plus a lot of gooks." The major had grown into the common habit of classifying all Korean soldiers as "gooks," whether friendly or enemy.

"See that your sentries are on the alert, and that nobody gets too much sleep," warned Major Hickson, in parting.

"Very good, sir." Parkington saluted, by force of habit, into the darkness.

Sergeant Sloan, who had been standing at his elbow, turned away to brief the platoon for the night guard.

"Better turn in now, sergeant," Parkington called after him. "I'll give you a shout about two, and you can take over until stand-to."

Sloan replied, gruffly, "That's O.K., sir; I'll do the first stag. I had a good kip in the train."

"Righto, then . . . thanks. I'll turn in first. Best let the chaps know what the position is, and it'll be a fifty-per-cent. turn-out."

Parkington slipped into his dugout, fully clothed, and pulled the blankets over him. Through the trees overhead the stars were visible, each outlined in a frosty halo. Thawing snow from an overladen branch above his head dripped constantly into the dugout, pattering on his waterproof poncho and running down in little rivulets on to the blankets. He was soon asleep.

Sloan had deployed half the platoon in the slit trenches, and himself occupied a trench on the right flank of the platoon area. It had stopped snowing. Through the sparse firs on either side he could see an occasional shadowy figure move in the area of other platoons. The trench overlooked a distant section of the main supply route, which was blazing with headlights as thousands of vehicles loaded with men and equipment flowed south out of the vast trap the Chinese had sprung. The muffled roar of engines was borne across on the night breeze. Nothing else stirred, apart from the occasional crunch of the gravel as he shifted his feet. He thought: When that column of traffic comes to an end this will be the front line.

Promptly, as the dial of his watch showed two o'clock, he went to wake Parkington. It was the longest four hours he had spent in his whole life.

But Sloan's reflections were not to achieve reality. During the morning, after the freezing ordeal of the hour's stand-to in the grey dawn, when huge fires were lit from timber torn from the wreckage of a derelict barn, the order came to pack up and move to a new location. Once more the frantic hurry to work to a set time, as the lorries arrived to be crammed with stores and equipment. At noon the battalion marched in column into the stream of traffic still moving south along the supply route, and turned towards Pyongyang, where they took up defensive positions commanding a bridgehead over the Taedong river. It was clear that the Northern capital was to be abandoned in face of the advancing Chinese armies. The task allotted to the 29th Brigade was to see the tail of the allied armies safely through the city, and then to pull out to positions farther south; if there was time.

Soon the battalion was steadily digging new defences along a ridge running parallel to the river, overlooking a plain which contained the airport. Here they remained for two days, while the stream of traffic pouring through the town declined to a trickle, and finally to nothing at all. . . .

During the second day the battalion moved out in a long convoy of lorries.

Mr Parkington, whose platoon was leaguered near a small copse of firs in a forward position, had received this message from his Company Commander. "The battalion will commence to withdraw from the present position at 2400 hours. Your platoon will cover the river-crossing during the withdrawal, and will be the last to leave. Your orders to withdraw will be signalled from Battalion Tactical H.Q. at approx. 0130 hours. You will not leave until you receive this notification, and you will then proceed to the battalion assembly-point as indicated on your map. . . ."

After the last company had gone through there was no traffic on the road apart from an occasional straggler.

During the afternoon the R.U.R.'s had left their position over the river, and the 25-pounders and the Centurion tanks had rumbled away in their wake.

Across the Taedong river the city of Pyongyang was disintegrating into smoke and ruin. Intermittent explosions occurred of ammunition stockpiles outside the city perimeter, like a display of carnival fireworks. Farther along the river the whole waterfront danced with the glow of great fires which brought into sharp relief warehouses, outlined against the background of a clear sky pimpled with bright stars. In the east, where an ammunition dump had been fired, balls of white fire streaked far into the night sky. The whole city was burning; the thin crackling of the flames carried across the river to the little knot of men clustered around the camp-fire on the north bank. The acrid tang of burning oil was blown across to them on the night air, cloying their nostrils.

B-29

Every few seconds now came the ponderous beat of powerful engines as all types of aircraft took off from the adjacent airfield, bearing south, gaunt and momentary shadows under a brilliant sky, glowing with fire. Already a myriad of smaller fires were springing up all over the airfield, and flames suddenly sprouted from a giant B-29 bomber lying crippled at the end of the runway. Now a hangar was enveloped in fire, spurting a vivid onion-shape of orange flame.

IV

THE RETREAT CONTINUES

After 1 A.M., when the last of the companies had gone, it was ominously peaceful. Everybody talked, not in whispers, but in the subdued voices which men use when they are not mentally at ease. Sergeant Sloan, sitting on a ration-box, was silently ruminating, biting on the stem of a heavily corroded briar which had long since ceased to emit smoke. Parkington attempted to pursue a spirited conversation with a small group of his men, but evoked so little response that he was left with the feeling that they were better left to their own thoughts. He glanced frequently at his watch as the hands advanced inexorably towards the hour of three. During the day Sergeant Sloan and Hurst had toured the doomed city in the three-ton Bedford. They drove through the side-streets, avoiding the main stream of traffic, pulling in to an American Stores Depot near the station.

"If you see anything you want, jus' take it, brother," said an officer in answer to Sloan's inquiry. "We're blowing the whole goddam issue in half an hour, so nobody's going to miss it."

So they had piled a load of clothing and boots on to the lorry, and went off hurriedly to another dump, where thousands of boxes of rations and cigarettes were about to be destroyed. They returned to the platoon area just after dark with a full load of loot, and the spoils were distributed on the spot.

Three o'clock, and the city flaring like a brand. . . . On the main supply route only the lights of an occasional straggler. The platoon were clustered in a circle around the large bonfire they had built. Only Woodbridge was unaware of the prickly silence; he was lost in the contemplation of a historical allusion involving a group of Roman legionaries watching the destruction of Carthage at a safe distance. There was little conversation. Anxiety showed in the men's eyes. Powell sat a little apart with his radio-set, headphones on, awaiting the signal to move.

The city had been officially given up at midnight. Already, in the campaign maps of the world, it would be shown as having fallen into Chinese hands. "Don't reckon they've forgot all about us, do you, sir?" some one had asked Parkington, and, indeed, he was beginning to feel jumpy himself. A movement in the shadows of the trees behind caused him to half withdraw his pistol. He was joined a moment later by an officer of the Artillery.

"What-oh!" he shouted cheerily. "What's this li'l outfit?" He wore a strange garb consisting of an American pile-jacket fastened tight over camouflaged windproofs, leather jackboots, fur cap with the ear-flaps hanging adrift, and a bright scarlet neck-wrap which had been issued originally as an air identification panel for vehicles. A ragged moustache climbing over bloated features completed for Parkington the illusion that he was confronted by some form of abominable snowman.

"Cap'narris," he announced breathlessly. "Pleased meet-cha. Got drop'a petrol? Got left b'hind, rear party; rest battery miles away. Now run out petrol. Jeep. 'Kin nuisance. Whew!"

"I think we can help you out," said Parkington. "Hurst, get a couple of cans of petrol and go with Captain Harris."

"Oh, marv'lous! In'scribably generous. Saved me life. What name, old boy?"

"Parkington. Gloucesters."

"Good-oh! Splendid! See you 'na minute. C'mon, Hurst." They were gone for several minutes, and then came lurching back over the adjacent paddy-fields in a jeep.

Captain Harris jumped out, brandishing a whisky-bottle, and joined the group at the fire. "Good show! Glorious blaze! Anybody care to have a nip?"

At first nobody offered.

"First man to speak up does the washing-up after," Harris said, looking ferociously round the circle.

Lane was the first to reply.

"Doan say as Oi indulges a lot," he said weightily, "but Oi never says no when anybody twists me arm."

There was general laughter, easing the tension. Lane's innocuous humour seemed totally incompatible with the fact that the Chinese had last been reported three miles to the north. That at any moment there might be a footfall, a shot. . . .

"Good man," Harris said. "Pass it round." Turning to Parkington, he said quietly, "When are you hitting the trail, chum?"

"Soon as we get the signal. Any moment now."

"Well, you'd better get a wriggle on. Bridge will be going up soon. Then where will you be?"

Parkington made no reply.

"I'll hang on until you go and follow you out. Haven't a clue where the rest of the battery are." Returning to the platoon, he said, "Dunno if you've heard this one, blokes. Stop me if you have. It's about a D.D.M.S.—that's Deputy Director of Medical Services—going on an inspection tour of a military hospital, see what I mean? Well, he gets to the first chap . . ."

"It were on the first night o' their 'oneymoon," Lane said.

"So this 'ere ginger geezer gits up and sez . . ."

"Hallo, narcotic one-zero. Six for one-zero . . ." Powell, the signaller, lying beside his set, now sat up and began to scribble a message on his pad, nodding his head in the affirmative. There was no need to read it. Parkington said, "Start up." Hurst and the two carrier-drivers ran to their driving-seats. Everybody scrambled aboard, cheering. The first carrier drew away and bumped over the rough track over the airfield down to the river-crossing, the remainder following. At the bridge a handful of tensed Americans watched them across. An officer shouted, "Step on it, you guys. We ain't got all night to stick around."

The little column moved on into the burning streets of the city. It was deserted now. Fire had

American 2½ Ton

seized control and was roaring avidly towards an early conquest. The air was thick with flying sparks and cinders. Parkington, in the leading carrier, ordered the driver to get through the city as quickly as possible. A booming explosion announced the destruction of the last bridge over the Taedong river. Whole streets were ablaze. It was hot inside the vehicles. "Warmest I've been since the Red Sea," mused Hurst, taking a sharp corner at a dangerous speed.

Showers of sparks and flaming fragments whirled high above the blazing buildings. The light over the city was broken by moving black masses of shadow. Gusts of warm air swept through the streets. The great white bulk of the municipal buildings shivered through a haze of red smoke, throwing into sharp relief a giant advertisement of a voluptuous Japanese actress outside a cinema opposite.

Intermittent explosions from blazing stockpiles

of ammunition rocked the area. At one street-crossing, where a munition-dump was burning, bullets hummed and skipped about on the road surface, one of them screeching through the canopy of the three-tonner, just above Powell's head.

Finally, the burning capital was behind them, and they were driving on down the road to the south. The headlights of the vehicles picked out scores of refugees straggling along at the road's edges, away from the recent disaster.

Hurst, driving the three-ton Bedford, was last in the convoy. Corporal Woodbridge was sitting beside him in the cab, and Powell was sitting on the platoon equipment, in the back. Two miles outside Pyongyang the engine spluttered, faded, picked up again, and stopped.

"Not nah!" Hurst pleaded. "Everything 'appens to Charlie." He jumped out and lifted the engine-cover. After a few minutes: "Carburettor's choked. 'Ave to get a tow, or else it's rice for breakfast."

By this time there was scarcely any traffic on the road. The American 2½-ton G.M.C. which suddenly and swiftly approached from the north, was probably their last chance. They stopped it. Woodbridge asked, "Can you give us a tow?" The driver, a small, excitable-looking Latin with a Bronx accent, shouted, "Okay, bud, but Ah'm in a goddam hurry, so youse'll have to hang on." Hurst quickly fixed a tow-rope.

The U.S. truck started off abruptly, so that the short rope grew suddenly taut, and the Bedford moved off with a sickening lurch. The next half-hour passed like a nightmare.

The lorry in front roared through the darkness at a suicidal speed, and Hurst's truck, at the end of the short rope, swayed from side to side of the road, which had become deeply rutted from the great weight of traffic which had passed through in the preceding week. The only indication of a turn was a slight decrease of speed in the American lorry. At one point Hurst sheered past an abandoned tank by inches; at another the two lorries swayed across a narrow bridge, which he negotiated by a narrower margin. After a stiff climb to the top of a ravine, and a breakneck run downhill, the Bedford, for several agonizing seconds, clung to the lip of the road, which fell away on the near side into a sixty-foot chasm. Woodbridge felt the hair rise on the nape of his neck, and sweat moistened his eyebrows in spite of the penetrating cold.

Hurst stared rigidly in front, using all his skill to fight off disaster. Behind them, in the back of the lorry, the signaller had fallen into a fitful sleep, in which he persisted despite the discomfort of being thrown about between shifting mounds of kit.

The journey had a dramatic ending. The leading truck swerved abruptly, and slowed to a halt. Hurst, desperately treading his brake-pedal, had a glimpse of a dark smudge on the road, under his wheels. A hundred yards farther on both trucks halted.

The U.S. driver leaped out of his cab and hammered on the windscreen of the lorry behind.

"Hey!" he shouted. "There's some old dame..."

"I know," Hurst said. The stress of recent events

had left him dazed; he felt aloof, and strangely unmoved. Woodbridge climbed slowly down over the running-board. "Let's go and see," he suggested.

"Sure. Let's go," the American driver said nervously. The lines of his features, etched in heavy ridges of dust, showed a turmoil of rage and fear and remorse. Together they walked back along the road to the body of a woman huddled against the bank.

She had been a very old woman. In life, it was evident from the emaciated condition of the body, from the tiny wrinkles which were like a network of gossamer over her sucked-in cheeks, she would have very quickly died from starvation.

The American spat decisively on the road. "The goddam bitch! How the heck do I see this old dame come at me?" He spread his hands in a gesture of appeal, and covered his face with them. Woodbridge, looking into the far distance, said, "Forget it. It wasn't your fault. Let's wrap her in a blanket, and put her out of sight."

This they did. Neither spoke again until the corpse of the old woman was discreetly wrapped in a blanket and laid in a hollow near the road. The little driver worked with willing persuasion, as if attending to the last rites of a relative in a New York tenement. As they walked back to the trucks he said in a low voice, "First time I ever killed anybody. That's all."

Woodbridge, looking vaguely at the stars, murmured a quotation:

"One thing is certain, and the Rest is Lies;
The flower that once hath blown for ever dies."

"Jeez," exclaimed the American, "Ah ain't never heard it expressed thataway!"

Hurst, working on the engine, had repaired the fault, and the Bedford continued under its own power. He remained quietly ruminative until they were several miles farther along the road. Then he asked, cryptically, "Dead?"

Woodbridge replied briefly in the affirmative. That was the last time they discussed the affair.

Powell had slept soundly throughout.

When they reached the battalion assembly area it was still dark. Hurst pulled in behind a line of trucks which stood nose to tail, their tail-lights glowing as far down the road as the eye could follow. Woodbridge climbed wearily on to the road, the intense cold having stiffened his muscles to a degree which made the operation an ordeal. Several figures were grouped around a fire on the far side, which had been made by setting light to a tyre soused with petrol. The glare of it flickered on drawn faces which had not been shaved.

Woodbridge went over and stood beside the fire, drawing in its heat, not caring about the oily smoke which belched from the tyre. His ears, while his body thawed, picked up the threads of several desultory conversations. On the fringe of the darkness the burning tyre was hemmed in by a jostling crowd.

"Yes, we just got that Centurion out in time." A tank officer was talking excitedly to some one whose face was withdrawn. ". . . just got it out in bloody time, and the other one had to go. Only one track thrown, forty thousand quid's worth, two hours' job, but the Yanks blew it. I tell you, the crew were going crazy. . . . And then I had to report to Brigade, mind you, and didn't even know where the hell they were, but I ran into a chap I've known for ages, name of Digger Green, at the crossroads, large as life, directing the traffic with an old-school scarf on. Recognized him at once, of course. You meet all sorts of types. Only last week . . ."

A duffel-coated bulk next to Woodbridge laughed cynically. "I must tell you this; met a young cavalry officer, just come out, very well-bred, Winchester and New and all that, stops me when we were halted at Suwon to ask where the latrines were, so I passed him on to a Yank, and the Yank showed him a paddy-field where about a dozen other Yanks were doing their stuff. And cold? It was worse than it is now. 'Go ahead,' this Yank says, 'there's plenty of room'; and this poor chap comes back livid and says, 'God, some of these people would crap under the clock in Victoria Station if they had the chance!'"

The falsetto laughter came again; the tyre flared and crackled with a fierce vigour. Now and then through the ruck of conversation came the rapid inflection of a foreign tongue and the lazy drawl of the American. Eventually a hoarse and authoritative shout from near at hand had the momentary effect of interrupting all discourse. "Hoi, you'll have to put that fire out. Haven't you chaps heard of a blackout?"

Gradually the officers drifted away, and the nucleus of men crouched even closer to the spluttering tyre, now dying out in a welter of swirling soot.

Finally they too were dispersed in a more persuasive manner. "You. Put that bloody fire out. How many more times d'you want telling?"

Some one stirred the embers with a boot, and the figures drifted away into the darkness and the relentless cold, filling the air with their complaints.

"Why doesn't somebody shoot the miserable bastard?"

"Come all the ——ing way out 'ere for ——all in the freezing ——ing cold, and yer can't even stand round a ——ing fire."

It was true that the possibility of enemy air-raids was practically non-existent. From a near-by camping plot the darkness was pierced by the glare of an acetylene torch where an American service unit was working all night on emergency repairs.

Woodbridge climbed back into the cab of the lorry, where Hurst was asleep, and adjusted his limbs into the least cramped position. He was very tired, and it was five o'clock, but he was too uncomfortable to sleep. An hour later he watched the icy dawn breaking over the hills, through the windscreen of the lorry.

V

"COMPO VALLEY"

The objective of the 29th Brigade during the retreat was to defend the rear of the armies rolling back on the west sector in a series of leap-frogging movements. After the evacuation of Pyongyang the Gloucesters retired sixty miles to the area of Sinmak, overtaking the rearguard elements of some of the retreating forces.

Below the snow-covered slopes where defensive positions were once again dug lay the small village of Congsok-tu-ri. The squalid habitations of the villagers were intact, but deserted. Here an epidemic of smallpox had swept through like a hot breath, claiming a third of those who had lived there. The remainder had fled, joining the ever-increasing hordes of refugees pouring south, leaving the rice-crop standing in the field until it had ripened and blown and wilted before the carping frosts of late autumn.

But after two days came the order to retreat once more, and the battalion leaguered again north of Kaesong, where after one night the vehicles and carriers once more pointed their noses south, to rattle through the streets of the silent city of Kaesong.

Those of the inhabitants who were too old, or too young, or too infirm, to begin the bitter trek to Pusan stared vacantly at the last of the retreating troops and retired to their already war-visited homes to await the arrival of the Chinese with the resignation of the Oriental. And as the endless columns of U.N. Army vehicles poured into the teeming, sprawling South capital of Seoul the advance units of the Chinese Communist forces crossed the Imjin river and infiltrated across the 38th Parallel.

They came mostly on foot; a number rode mules. There were few vehicles. The retreating armies had left a legacy of broken bridges and shattered railways in their wake.

So far, apart from an occasional salvo of long-range artillery, no shot had been exchanged during the retreat in the west by the opposing ground forces, but from the airfields far to the south swarms of U.S. fighters roared overhead to strafe the advancing Chinese with rockets and napalm.

By this time the troops were becoming acclimatized.

Lessons they had learned in Africa, in Italy, in the jungle of Burma, sleeping under trucks, in ditches and trees, and in the open, working, sweating, fighting in steaming jungles, over hot sands and on icy, barren plains—to these lessons were added new ones every day. There were men like Hurst who had lived hard enough to find luxury in a roll of blankets and a groundsheet, who could sleep as soundly when the air vibrated with the noise of shells as when all was silence, and would waken at a touch and be instantly one hundred per cent alive. And the leavening of newcomers to war like Woodbridge and Parkington suffered more, but they learnt more because of stark necessity, and because they had more to learn; and they were taught by able mentors.

It was nothing but the breaking down of routine to the barest simple necessity—like keeping warm all the time, and eating when you were hungry, and knowing how to dig your foxhole quickly and economically, wasting no effort; it was having a roof which did not leak, making a fire which would last and give a strong heat. It was in not carting chairs about in your truck until you finally realized that you had spent more time in carrying them than in sitting on them.

It was this flexible routine of half discipline and half self-preservation which maintained the orderliness of the retreat in its bitterest moments.

It was on December the 16th that the brigade arrived to take up new positions seven miles to the north of Seoul to await the oncoming Chinese. The defence positions spread along a valley pent in by towering hills, running off from the main supply route to the north. It was christened "Compo Valley" after the composite rations which were brought up each day in crates from the railhead, and consisted of stringy bacon, corned beef, soya sausages, steak-and-kidney pudding, dehydrated potatoes, and very little else. Some one, either a pessimist or a prophet, called it the Valley of Death.

The platoons, thinly scattered over the hillsides, began digging in. Across the main supply route, the U.S. 25th Div. were digging in on the left flank, farther to the north, and on the right were the British 27th Brigade, which had pulled out through Pyongyang after fighting on the Manchurian border. Of the 29th Brigade, the Ulsters and Northumberlands were forward, and the Gloucesters, in the rear, held the centre.

The battalion were in Corps Reserve, which meant a general lessening of tension.

For Parkington this was the time of the shooting of the Korean prisoners. Soon after the battalion had established itself a sentry reported three strange vehicles passing behind the battalion positions, along a track which crossed a wide re-entrant running into the high ridge where Parkington's platoon commanded a point of vantage. Parkington and Sloan, going to the far side of the hill to investigate, observed the three lorries winding slowly along in a small cloud of dust, a thousand feet below. "They're Koreans all right," said Parkington focusing his binoculars, "and they seem to be stopping."

"Police, I suppose," Sloan remarked. "There's thousands of them about, but they don't usually come up this far."

"They're all getting out now... about twenty of them on the truck behind, and... funny... looks as if their hands are tied together in pairs."

"Prisoners, maybe, brought up to dig defences?" Sloan suggested.

"Could be! The guards are all armed, anyway." Parkington followed with close attention the miniature figures now deploying themselves on the roadside.

"They're being shoved into some holes that look like weapon-pits...none too gently, either...My God, it looks as if they're going to be shot." The harsh rattle of carbine-fire gave a grim emphasis to his remarks.

"The guards are systematically shooting them all in the back of the head."

Sloan, without the aid of glasses, saw an old man, whose turn was next, defiantly shake a clenched fist in the air before crumbling like a deflated tyre over the lip of his grave, and another, much younger, wrap his arms round the ankles of his executioner. The rattle of gunfire was almost continuous now, but during the occasional breaks in it another sound drifted faintly over the hill. It was the screams of the dying, and the wailing of those about to die.

Parkington handed the binoculars to Sloan. "What d'you make of the pair on the end?"

Sloan said, "One looks like a woman, and the other, I should say, is a small boy."

"Exactly."

"Isn't there anything we can do to stop it?"

"I'm afraid it's too late." Parkington pointed down to the delta, where the noise had ceased and the guards were busy shovelling earth on to the bloodstained corpses.

They returned to the platoon area, and Parkington went to report to the Company Commander. Major Hickson, after listening to the details, said, "Yes... mmm," rapping his fingers on the edge of his table (which was a large ration-box) in a way he always affected while turning over in his mind the points of an especial problem. Finally, he said, "I can report it, but we'll probably be told that this is not our affair."

"But it's plain bloody murder, sir."

"Call it that if you like. I couldn't agree more. But it's really only a drop in a whole ocean of iniquity. I've heard something about these executions: the prisoners are political, suspected of Communist sympathies when Seoul was last occupied. Now that they think Seoul is likely to fall into Communist hands again they are making a clean sweep."

"And we can do nothing about it?"

"Nothing useful."

"It didn't seem much of a way to die, sir, that's all." Parkington turned to leave.

"I don't suppose it is," agreed Major Hickson. "But this isn't an old-school-tie war. It's a dirty, squalid, hole-in-the-corner business, and before the end of it you'll see a lot more things which you like even less than what you saw to-day."

Christmas 1950. . . .

Christmas was celebrated on the 24th of December by order of the brigadier, in case the Chinese, now drawing near in considerable strength, should take advantage of the festive season and attack on the 25th.

On this mock-Christmas morning the snow, which had persisted during the past month, still clung to the crags which surrounded the company area. In the midst of such desolation the scene was not without a certain unreal beauty. Towards midday the sun

struggled weakly through a layer of high cloud, and
the snow, which had frozen into hard crystals, became suddenly alive with a dazzling brilliance. Men
were busy about the company lines, and walking to
and fro rather aimlessly like ants, lost among their
memories of Christmases spent in happier times and
circumstances.

The first intimation of something foreign and
unexpected was the faint whining note which perco-
lated into the valley from the far distance, like an
echo, turning into a faint, muffled rhythm. The sound
grew in intensity, by slow degrees. It mounted;
weird, lonely, as doleful as surf crashing on to a
deserted beach. Gradually it flooded into the valley
and rolled across the hills.

Every man stopped to listen. Round the bend of
the road a squad of men in brown kilts were marching,
just as the bitter wind which had sprung up during
the morning subsided and the first gentle flurry of a
new snowfall settled.

It was the Irish pipes and drums of the Royal
Ulster Rifles.

As they approached the skirling music thudded
and vibrated against the brilliant white crags overhanging the valley—all the hills were ringing with a
sound to which they had never rung before; would
never again ring.

The pipes played *Mother Machree*, *Endearing
Young Charms*, and departed to the cadence of a
lively jig, like the creatures of a fantastic mirage,
leaving the tuneful lilt of their music echoing in the
ears of every man.

The interlude provided a sharp boost to morale

generally. There was a quickening of the tread, and the spirit of Christmas, which was previously obscure and unalive in this barren place, now became real and tangible, after all.

For several days previously the sergeant-major and the colour-sergeant, with a handful of helpers, had been preparing for the Christmas festivities. In a large tent loaned by a friendly American unit, pitched in the centre of the company area, a number of ready-made tables had been erected, with ration-boxes to sit on. All day the cooks slaved with their ovens improvised out of petrol-drums let into the clay, roasting the turkeys which had been thoughtfully provided with the previous day's rations.

The sergeant-major made a rum punch from tins of American fruit-cocktail and carefully conserved rum rations. Oranges were also provided.

The feast was to be followed by a 'party,' and a supply of tinned beer had been laid by for free consumption. A piano,—a mildewed and battered instrument salvaged from Seoul's ruins, with the panelling torn from the face of it to reveal the strings as gaunt as the rib-bones of a desecrated corpse—stood at one end of the tent, which was inadequately lit by four twelve-volt headlight bulbs running on a charging engine which coughed and spluttered interminably outside.

Standing near the entrance was the lopped-off crown of a fir-tree—a Christmas tree, stuck in an oil-drum, decorated with silver paper saved from packets of chocolate. Two more petrol-drums with stove-piping fashioned from shell containers had been inserted to serve as wood fires.

At eight o'clock the first of the two sittings for dinner commenced. The men streamed down from the hill positions, leaving a few sentries on guard. The turkeys were brought in to a great ovation by Sloan and his fellow platoon sergeants, Webb and Benson, who subsequently served dinner to the men. Major Hickson carved with a borrowed bayonet. For an hour afterwards knives and forks grated against mess-tins. By ten o'clock the proceedings were well under way.

Captain Mason performed creditably on the piano, which proved surprisingly mellow and agreeable in spite of the drawback of several missing notes. Several carols were sung with a gusto which threatened to shake the tent from its moorings.

Caps of beer containers popped on all sides. Empties littered the floor, mingling with orange-peel, cigar-butts, and an assortment of coloured paper. From a mysterious source some one produced a bundle of paper hats, which set the true seal of carnival on the wearers.

The wood fires roared and crackled and were replenished, glowing red-hot to the stack-pipes. Fumes of tobacco and wood rose in a bank of blue vapour to the tent roof, to hang there in a solid pall. The dim lights gleamed dully.

A cook in greasy white overalls shuffled forward with an air of furtive truculence and began to sing *Long Ago and Far Away* in a loud, coarse voice which vulgarly caressed the words in a manner emulating a certain famous and voluptuous torch-singer. Jeers and cheers alike greeted the end of each verse, particularly at the conclusion of the song, when the cook shuffled back to his corner with the same expressionless demeanour.

Now it was Hurst's turn. During the evening he had been drinking rum, and holding an animated conversation with a small clique of drivers drawn from other platoons. Every now and again his ringing laughter, tumbling down from a high treble, cut across the hum of conversation like the grate of a power-driven saw tearing into unseasoned pitch-pine. He took the cook's place in the centre of the arena and roared for silence. The hubbub receded noticeably. "Listen!" he bawled. "Liss–en!"

Comparative silence. . . .

"Nah, listen, blokes, I'm goin' ter say a few kind words about the sargint-may-jah."

Enormous cheers from the assembly. A bleak smile from the sergeant-major. . . .

"Quiet! As you all know, the old cock 'as done us very well, makin' all the arrangements for a slap-up do ter-night, which, as you all know, is Ker-ristmas night. Okay?"

Cheers. . . . A shout of "Wot a geezer!"

"So as a littal tribute from all of us to all of 'im . . ."

Roars of approbation . . . the sergeant-major's smile positively wintry. . . .

"Nah, 'old it. I'm goin' to sing a littal song which 'as been spesh'ly written an' dedicated to the sar-gint-may-jah."

Another outburst, dying away to near-silence. . . .

Hurst cleared his throat ostentatiously. His song was delivered in a throaty roar which rose above the raucous demonstrations of his audience:

> *"You've got a kind face, you old bastard;*
> *You ought to be bleedin'-well shot.*
> *You ought to be chained to a dung-'eap,*
> *An' left there to bleedin'-well rot.*
> *You ought to be tarred an' fevvered . . ."*

At this point the noise became so tumultuous that the rest of Hurst's words were drowned, and the sergeant-major was enthusiastically hoisted on a multitude of shoulders and chaired round the tent in triumph.

Parkington and Gilmour had been talking to a young American lieutenant, Eagan, who was a liaison officer with the 29th Brigade.

Eagan, who was slightly drunk, was saying. "Too much reserve, the British, that's what they tell me, an' here's a couple hunnerd guys all shouting their heads off."

"It's just the circumstances," laughed Gilmour. "You ought to see them back in England in the local pubs where they belong. They'd freeze you."

"Know what I think?" pursued Eagan. "I rec'n these guys are all yellin' their heads off because they wanna forget about sump'n."

"Or perhaps it's because they're trying not to remember," Parkington suggested.

"You wanna know what I rec'n?" continued the

American. "I rec'n behind all that blowin' of their tops there is jus' one liddle thing, an' one only, which is always on their minds. Know what it is?"

"The Chinese," Parkington offered glibly.

"Whichese?"

"The boat back home?"

"No, siree. You guys are away off the beam. The one thing these guys miss most of all because they cain't get it here . . ."

"Mine," broke in Gilmour, "has got mousy-coloured hair and a pretty good figure and a vile habit of making up in public."

"Mine's red-headed. Lousiest little floozie in Philadelphia, with one hell of a come-to-bed smile. Guess I'd walk all the way from Los Angeles just to watch it come on at that, right this minute. . . ."

"Come on, Charlie-boy. Let's hear all about your popsie," Gilmour said.

The celebration broke up in the early hours of the morning, and the men wandered out of the tent in little groups, to stumble awkwardly through the darkness to their own bivouacs, flushed to a pleasant warmth by the rum inside them and the effect of the rank cigars which had been supplied in plentiful numbers by a trio of guests—American drivers from the all-black trucking company camped near by.

VI

FIRST CONTACT

What were the Chinese going to do?

In some quarters hope was held out that, having retaken the whole of North Korea, they would be content to rest on the laurels of this easy conquest; that they would come no farther than the 38th Parallel.

Occasionally the artillery grouped around the Brigade H.Q. would fire a salvo, shattering the peace which brooded all along the valley. Patrols which were sent out to probe the forward areas returned with no information, but the spotting planes brought back ominous reports of heavy troop concentrations massing along the border.

In the minds of the troops existed a constant vision, not of conquest, but of home.

"When are we going home?" It was the leading question that men asked, growing so familiar that it became a form of greeting. "'Allo, Nobby; when are we goin' 'ome, mate?"

"Never, mate. Cold, ain't it?"

Cold it certainly was.

Unobtrusively the old year slipped away and died, and the winter tightened its grip. In their

Vickers Gun

exposed position high in the hills the Vickers guns froze, and the water in their jackets became solid blocks of ice. In the tanks of the vehicles the anti-freeze liquid froze. Sleeping-bags were sent up from Base Stores and were distributed. To be able to slip into their fleecy, quilted interior was indeed a luxury compared with the cold comfort of four blankets; blankets which it was impossible to arrange in such a way that they cut out the entry of piercing draughts, and at the same time provided an adequate covering for the body.

It was New Year's Eve.

Sloan and Woodbridge celebrated in their bivouac. The bivouac was a shack made of odd-shaped pieces of canvas thrown across a rough wooden framework held together by four poles which formed the corner posts. A fifth pole in the centre held up the sagging roof. The canvas was staked to the ground. At one point it did not reach, and the consequent gap was bridged by ammunition-boxes, which served also as seats. The shack was almost waterproof; it was quite roomy, and strong enough to withstand all but the hardest gales. A stove had been erected in one corner, and sufficient wood to last the evening had been painstakingly collected.

The guests arrived during the early evening. They consisted of Powell, Lane, Hurst, Cave, and two Americans—Hump, the cook sergeant, and Henry, one of the Negro drivers from the trucking company.

Cave was the platoon's rumour-monger. He was a tall, steely-eyed man with a shock of dark frizzed hair who seemed to shed rumours like a dog shakes off water after falling into a canal.

"What's the latest rumour, Cavey?" some one would ask, and he never disappointed them or repeated the same fabrication twice. He would proclaim them spontaneously, and with apparent sincerity, radiating truth, so that nobody ever really knew whether he actually believed them himself.

"When are we going home, Cavey?"

"February. So they say. The bloke as does batman to the major on the staff up at Brigade read it the other day in a letter on 'is table, according to the R.A.S.C. driver as comes up wi' the P.O.L. lorry. We'm bein' relieved. 19th Brigade just goin' through the Suez now in the *Orwell*, accordin' to a bloke in

Dog wot sez 'e as a brother wot was on it. 'Ad a letter only last week."

Even when he announced, "The Yanks is goin' to push us all back to Formosa, because public opinion at 'ome is all agin us stayin' out here," some almost believed.

Woodbridge had produced a cocktail for the occasion from all the strong liquor available. He called it "Peking Paramour." The ingredients were gin, whisky, rum, orange-juice, saké, and evaporated milk. The mixture looked and smelt like a very potent metal-polish.

It was poured out into mugs, and passed round. Woodbridge sat back to watch the reaction. The cook sergeant was the first to drink.

Hump was a large and rotund Negro with a shining moonface and an air of perpetual merriment. He raised the mug, pursing his pale lips, and quickly tilted it, pouring a good measure of the liquid into his throat.

His eyes dilated, slowly widening. His lips quivered; his great torso heaved and shuddered. With a spontaneous movement one huge hand flew to his throat as if it had received an urgent summons there. For one moment his face registered acute surprise, then relaxed into soft lines of contentment. He withdrew his hand, and once again sought the handle of the mug.

"Wow! That is shoh some stuff," he said emphatically.

Sloan disposed of his without fuss, quietly, as a hardened drinker. Hurst, after spitting out the first mouthful with an oath, returned to attack the remainder with forced relish. The other Negro, Henry, looked at the turgid liquid with horror, and drained it with the air of a martyr. Later he was sick.

Lane, after taking a tentative sip, put his mug down and slyly disposed of the contents outside afterwards, and Cave, who was no drinker, did the same.

Nevertheless "Peking Paramour" was voted an outstanding success.

The evening passed in congenial fashion. The fire roared hungrily, and showers of sparks crackled in the stovepipe, and shot out into the night. The pressure-lamp kept up a steady popping, and Woodbridge pumped it vigorously and frequently, while Hurst related some details of his former life.

"Remember once I 'ad a job doin' a baker's round," he said. "One place there's a very nice piece 'oo is always giving me the eye, so one day I goes inside an' starts givin' 'er the old routine, see..."

"What about her husband?" Sloan inquired caustically.

"'E was in the next room listenin' to a play on the wireless, an' she calls out to him. 'Darling,' she says, 'the baker is assaultin' me.' He calls out, 'Just a moment, dear, the play is just approaching its climax,' an' she says, 'So is the baker.' Women are all the same," pronounced Hurst, "only some not so much as the uvvers. Like a tart I once picked up down 'Ackney way..."

The conversation was punctuated by the big Negro's raucous belly-laughter, which was distributed generously. He sat in one corner, saying little, but laughing nearly all the time.

Cigars were passed around with fresh portions of "Peking Paramour." Sloan puffed contentedly at his pipe, which was filled with plug tobacco which he had purchased on the troopship. It gave off a tang of burning dung. Nobody cared.

"I suppose you've 'eard about the big push?" Cave asked. "One of the corporals down at Field Ambulance got it from an Intelligence Orficer wot was brought in for inoculations. Chinese are supposed to be ready for a big push wot is startin' to-night. Zero hour is midnight."

"That's rather awkward," Woodbridge said. Turning to Henry, he asked, "What would you do if the Chinese came to-night, Henry?"

The little man's eyes rolled, so that only the whites were visible. "Jeez!" he exclaimed. "If dose Chinese come Ah jus' ain't gonna be here, Ah rec'n."

As Sloan's watch showed midnight they crawled out of the shack into the brilliant starlit night, under a bitter sky, and howled *Auld Lang Syne* at the moon in concert, grouped in a semicircle. They sang the familiar words like they had never sung them before, and the echo of their voices mingled with the echoes of other voices from farther up the valley, for tradition dies hard, and particularly sentimental tradition.

Later the two Americans stumbled away, the big cook helping the small driver, who looked pale and ill, with the ring and boom of the former's laughter carrying back until he was out of earshot. Woodbridge, who had taken more of his own evil mixture than he intended, became suddenly drowsy, clasped hold of the central pole of the shack, and slid gracefully down it to the ground. Some one thoughtfully threw a blanket over him. He went to sleep at once. Four hours later he woke up, colder than he had ever been before, and with a great effort undressed and struggled into his sleeping-bag.

Hurst had to be taken to his own dugout by Lane and Powell; at first he refused to be led there, saying it was not his.

"Take me back ter dear ol' Blighty," he sang in a quavering voice.

"D-don't be a ber-loody f-fool," Powell said, stuttering more than usual. "This is Ker-ker-Korea, not Blighty."

"Back ter Blighty," insisted Hurst.

"All right, you'm goin' back on the boat now," Lane said soothingly. "Watch your feet on the gangplank." He negotiated Hurst's stumbling footsteps over a tricky area full of concealed trenches.

"Tha's right," Powell said. "Now watch yerself goin' down the stairs to the c-cabins." He caught Hurst's arm just in time to prevent him from falling.

"Where'sh the stewardeshes?" Hurst demanded to know.

"Oi'll be sendin' a couple down. Here's the door," forcing Hurst into the entrance of their communal bivouac, a trench cut into the side of the hill, and covered with corrugated iron and sacking.

"Now up into the bunk"—with a concerted effort they forced Hurst bodily on to his camp-bed—"an' in the mornin' ye'll be on the way to Blighty."

"'Ar. If 'e's ——in' lucky," Powell said, as he turned to go back to his own sleeping-bag.

"Sh'all I care. Blighty isha pashe for me..." mumbled Hurst. He turned over and began to snore loudly.

As Lane prepared to get into bed a sentry appeared outside, pointed at Hurst, and said, "Tell 'im 'e's on in a few minutes, Laney."

Cursing softly under his breath, Lane groped for his greatcoat and rifle and disappeared, for the next two hours, into the night.

On the 4th of January the Chinese attack commenced on the Brigade front. All night the three battalions had stood-to, and in the morning positive reports of enemy groups in the immediate vicinity poured into Battalion H.Q., where the Intelligence Officer, sick of clutching at the straws of odd unidentified persons who always turned out to be harmlessly Korean, for weeks past, now became excited and alert, poring over his map-board.

During the morning the 25-pounders of the Royal Artillery opened up with the first salvo of a running barrage which continued all day to rain shells into the enemy positions as bearings flowed in from the observation points. At midday the Northumberland Fusiliers, securely entrenched on a commanding ridge, opened fire on a number of figures advancing along the hill paths; figures that were seen suddenly to change their garb from the white smock of the Korean peasant to the grey-green quilted kapok of the Chinese soldier.

The R.U.R.'s were engaged by small patrolling

forces during the afternoon, but still no shot was fired on the Gloucester front.

From Parkington's position which overlooked a misty panorama of rugged white peaks and winding rocky valleys only occasionally were small groups of Chinese seen through binoculars, well out of range; but forward the whole front was alive with the flashes of exploding shells, and the air was full of the distant crump of explosives and the rattle of small-arms fire.

In the centre of the Gloucester's lines the 4.2-inch mortars of 170 Battery were positioned. All day the gunners swung their blunt barrels on to new bearings, and a constant flow of bombs crashed from them and hummed across the intervening hills.

At a range of two miles a Chinese mortar team set up their battery to bombard the Brigade area. This they were seen to do by an R.A. observer officer high up on an O.P. Through the field telephone he relayed to the gunnery officer the precise range and bearing. For several minutes the 4.2's fell silent as the Chinese laboured to bring up the mortars and mount them in close proximity to each other on a rocky ledge, and then to bring up the ammunition and stack it beside the mountings.

"All right, they're ready. Let it go," crackled the voice on the telephone.

"One to six guns—fire!" bellowed the gunnery officer.

The six 4.2's barked with a single voice.

When the smoke cleared nothing could be seen of the opposing mortars or their crews, only a trickle of rubble which fell from the ledge where they had once been.

* * *

From their positions in the hills the two forward battalions picked off the advancing squads of Chinese with long-range small-arms fire. Towards nightfall the battle, which had never really started in earnest, subsided, while the Chinese withdrew to regroup, having found the opposition more severe than they had expected.

At four o'clock the U.S. 25th Division on the left flank, holding the road, withdrew and began to pull out along the road to Seoul.

And at nine o'clock, when the whole front was tensed and the forward areas were starkly delineated by the light of flares, the order to withdraw came to Brigade H.Q., and was urgently wirelessed to the Battalion Commanders. There was not much time left.

The Gloucesters began their withdrawal at ten o'clock.

Once again all the arms and ammunition and rations were dumped into the lorries and carriers; but this time only the bare essentials were carried. There was no time to load the accessories which the troops had collected during the campaign, such as wash-bowls, old batteries for lighting, battered Japanese stoves. . . . Even the bedding and cookhouse equipment were left, scattered over the hills. Canvas dwellings were left intact. An entire hot meal was left steaming in dixies to await the oncoming Chinese. In the straggling moonlight the trucks began to move off in a long line of retreat, packed with men who were seething with discomfort and bitterness. In the valley the narrow track which led to the main supply route was fast becoming churned into a morass of mud and slush over which the lorries lurched and slithered on locked wheels. There were many stoppages while men struggled to free vehicles which had slid off the road. Two carriers which became bogged down on the roadside had to be abandoned and blown up. As the slow-moving column reached the main supply route it was joined by the vehicles of the Artillery battery and the rear elements of the 25th Division, while the Royal Northumberland Fusiliers constituted the rear of the great caterpillar of traffic stretching beyond Seoul.

The Royal Ulster Rifles were the last battalion to retreat. Their column of vehicles took another route which joined the main supply route farther to the north.

Half-way along this route a strong force of Chinese had infiltrated to take up positions on a feature which commanded the track along which the Ulsters' column passed.

The two rear companies were ambushed.

The first intimation they had of the presence of the enemy was the rattle of machine-gun fire; a hail of bullets poured into their vehicles from the side of a hill; bugles sounded. A hill which two hours previously had been one in a dreary procession of loping mounds stretching far to the east now became alive with moving figures.

The two companies were trapped. They fought back. For half an hour there was a sharp and bloody encounter there in the valley which was called "Compo Valley." At the height of the action arrive the tanks of

Churchill Tank

Cooper force, a troop of supporting Churchills formed from the 7th Tank Regiment.

The Churchills roared into the centre of the valley with their quick-firers hurling shells into the side of the enemy-occupied hill, and deployed among the narrow paddy-fields by the side of the track.

The Chinese replied with intensive small-arms fire; they swarmed down from their positions on the hillside, shouting above the noise of battle for the Ulsters to surrender. The tanks slithered in the soft mud of the paddies, while their Besas sprayed out a swarm of bullets. Chinese dead piled up at the foot of the hill. Those that lived through the screen of lead that the tanks threw out swarmed on to the tanks themselves and fastened grenades in their tracks. The Churchills, immobile on the slippery terraces of the paddy-fields, could not regain the road. One of them, roaring and thrashing in a sea of mud of its own making, with Chinese clinging to the turret like bees on a honeycomb, finally overturned and lay with its unprotected belly uppermost, with its assailants crushed to a pulp underneath.

When, eventually, the battle ceased the carnage which had been wrought stared out of the eyes of the dead and the dying men, and was manifest in the blunt hulls of the silent and crippled tanks. The Ulsters had lost over two hundred.

But the remainder of the Brigade got safely away from "Compo Valley" and headed south once more towards the Han river.

Lane, hunched up in the corner of one of the carriers, listened to the bitter recriminations which went on around him.

"You spend a ruddy fortnight sitting behind a Bren with your eyes skinned, and as soon as you get a chance to let fly they give you about five minutes to get out. . . ."

"Roll on Pusan. Never been so cheesed off since I was in the nick, and then I 'ad a roof over me 'ead, and I did know 'ow long it was going to last. But out 'ere we could all rot until doomsday, and nobody ever giving a tinker's f—t."

"I wonder what slit-eyed yellow basket will be

kipping in my sleeping-bag to-night," growled a burly lance-corporal. "Whoever it is, he'll be a bloody sight better off than me."

"The one as sleeps in mine will find 'un a bit too warm, Oi reckon," said Lane. "Jus' 'fore Oi left Oi put a phosphorous grenade in 'ee, and tied the flap to the dam' thing."

VII

STANDING FIRM

Seoul, the sprawling capital of South Korea, is a city of two identities. The most poignant of these is assumed by the suburbs, where the mass of the inhabitants live jam-packed together in warrens of squalid hovels, where the territory of each is bounded by the four mud walls of its perimeter. Among these stinking jerry-built shacks an endless chapter of native life is written out in terms of pestilence and misery. There can be little change in the grey existence of these depressed areas which are spread all over the outskirts of the city, and the visitation of war served only to increase the squalor of their lot, by reducing the standards of the inhabitants to below the starvation level, on the borders of which they had previously survived.

The centre of Seoul, before it was shattered and polluted by occupying armies, was a majestic Oriental city where trams rattled along wide, well-surfaced streets which were bounded by impressive architecture of modern Japanese origin. The central station was a towering neo-Gothic structure. Buddhist temples studded the city; large monumental buildings straddled the road.

There was a district devoted to banks and official and municipal buildings built of white stone. Hotels stood quietly back in natural surroundings.

There must, once, have been gardens. . . .

But war has an easy conscience, and the Seoul through which the retreating Allied armies poured on that January night in 1951 was a ruined city.

It was a city of mounds of rubble, of windowless shop-fronts with boards nailed across. Of buildings half standing and half a crazy pattern of destruction, and of lofty edifices which at close quarters showed an ominous aspect of smoke-blackened and hollowed-out vacancy.

It was a city of dust, dust like sand which rose under the wheels of passing vehicles and settled in thick layers on window-ledges, on the broken chassis of abandoned vehicles; on deserted acres of broken masonry.

And during the retreat, when four lines of traffic crawled abreast through the main street leading to the bottleneck at the Han river crossing, the remaining inhabitants of Seoul knew that their city was doomed. Thousands fled.

The South Korean Government had issued instructions for a complete evacuation of the civilian population. Those who reached Pusan, the manifesto announced, would be conveyed to islands off the southern coast of Korea, there to begin a new life in a friendly land to which war was a stranger. Pusan was two hundred and eighty miles away. There was no transport.

On this occasion the stockpiles of military equipment in the city had been cleared in time, after the sharp lesson of Pyongyang. Only the heavy installations which were too cumbersome to dismantle remained to be destroyed, and these were blown up in accordance with a prepared policy of evacuation.

Intermittent fires glowed throughout the city. The airfield installations across the river were burning steadily, like great torches lighting the retreat.

The headlights of the jostling traffic made the streets as bright as a Piccadilly Saturday night. Through the maze of back-streets there moved fleeting shadows as the panicking refugees—women, children, old men—loaded with their pitiful belongings, moved down in a great concourse to the river Han, where they crossed over on the ice and followed the column of traffic along the main supply route to the south.

Parkington, in a jeep at the river's edge, waiting to see his vehicles safely on to the pontoon bridge which traversed the river, sat watching a haggard woman, a child bound to her back by a filthy sash, hacking a hole in the ice with the heel of her wooden clog. Two other children, scarcely of an age to walk, stood beside her, blue with cold, wailing continuously.

Parkington was totally unprepared for what happened next. The woman quickly untied the sash, grasped the baby by its armpits, and lowered it into the water. It made no sound. The turgid current below clutched at its emaciated body and dragged it under the surface of the ice. Quite without any semblance of emotion, she retreated with short, mechanical steps, followed by the remainder of her brood.

For a moment Parkington was stunned with horror at the sight; he was filled with dismay at his own impotence in the face of such tragedy. As the jeep moved on over the bridge he turned to Gilmour, sitting beside him in the back seat of the vehicle. He said, "Did you see . . . that?"

"Yes. What can you do?"

"Nothing," Parkington said.

"Nothing at all," Gilmour said. "And that's the hell of it."

Across the river, they approached the shattered industrial town of Yongdungpo, a prospect of tall chimneys reaching up stark against the skyline above the wreckage of factories and warehouses. Even at this hour the streets were filled with the thousands of refugees pouring in from Seoul to find shelter for the night among the ruined buildings, anywhere which would afford some protection from the paralysing cold, before they continued their long journey at daybreak.

Suwon again . . .

This time the battalion camped in the fields opposite the university buildings, which since their previous occupation had been devoured by fire and were now a burnt-out shell.

But this time the troops did not dig defensive positions. It was obvious that Suwon too was to be given up without a struggle; that in a short time the battalion vehicles would be warming up to head south again towards an unspecified destination.

Well—something was sure to happen soon. As

Cave, who was a great amateur strategist, pointed out with satisfaction, "It can't go on for ever. Couple more weeks o' this, an' they'll wake up an' find we'm up to our necks in salt water. Then I 'spect some one'll do sump'n."

The Gloucesters remained at Suwon for two days.

During this time Parkington was to witness another scene in the tragedy of the refugees.

On the second day he had been sent to Suwon railway station on the routine duty of arranging for the collection of a consignment of stores for the battalion. As his jeep approached the station the scene there was very little changed from the day that the battalion had detrained after their first move from Pusan. Parkington left the jeep and went through the station buildings to look for the office of the U.S. R.T.O.

Standing at the platform was a train—a long line of cattle-wagons occupied by Korean refugees. Although the train was full, it showed no sign of attempting to move. If the wagons were packed to solidity inside, and here and there Parkington saw the outline of bodies pressed hard against barred windows, they literally swarmed with humanity outside. Refugees hugging their miserable bundles were massed upon the roofs, swayed dangerously on the foot-boards, and hung like bats from the bars of the windows. As Parkington watched, the engineer and two firemen fought to repel an invasion of the cab, using their iron-shod boots as bludgeons on swaying heads.

The fetid stink of unwashed bodies, stale urine, and decaying garbage overhung the platform and lingered about the entrance to the whitewashed and creosoted office of the Railway Transport Officer.

He was not amused. He was telling a brother officer that these goddam refugees would be the death of him, just as he was about due to be rotated. He glanced up as Parkington walked in, and indicated the train with a thumb.

"That train has stood there for just thirty hours," he said. "And we can't get rid of it because the military stuff has the first priority, and there is only a single track on this railway. And even if I let it go," he explained, "most of those gooks won't get through the first tunnel."

"When the last train got as far as Chonan the guys there had to knock 'em off the outside with poles. Yessir, they were frozen on."

"Frozen on!" he repeated emphatically. "How d'ya like that?"

The Brigade's next position was in the vicinity of the town of Pyongtaek, where the Gloucesters dug their defensive line among the ruins of yet another village on the main supply route. Here the land was quite flat for several miles, and there was no cover, although the hills, never far in the background, were visible in the distance. The weapon-pits were sited among the pathetic remains of houses and small farms, several of which were still occupied, while several of the troops themselves occupied some of the vacant buildings which still stood after the inhabitants had fled. Sloan and Woodbridge made their home in the only habitable room of a primitive house shaped like a capital E with the centre-stroke missing. There was a thatched roof which sagged on top of the structure like an untidy hat. Inside, the room was papered with old newspaper which hung down in tattered shreds, revealing the bare mud walls supported by twisted beams. The ceiling, too, was of newspaper-sheets gummed together in thick wads, and there were a number of large rents in it.

Outside a crude kitchen had been built into the side of the house, like an outhouse, containing a range of three iron gratings let into a bank of clay to accommodate several large cooking-pots. A space for a wood-fire was hollowed out underneath. Sloan noticed that the holes extended underneath the floor of the house, and at the far side he found a stackpipe protruding from another bank of clay. He lit a fire in the entrance and watched the smoke gushing out of the stackpipe. The room began to warm up. Sloan piled on more fuel before settling down to a night's sleep among the straw which he had collected from a barn. Soon he felt drowsy and comfortable.

Woodbridge, coming in from a spell of guard duty, found him asleep. There was a smell of burning in the room, and in the corner a patch of straw was alight. Sloan's blankets were smouldering. The room was full of a stifling heat. . . .

During the next few days the battalion worked hard erecting barbed wire and minefields. Their position along the main supply route through which the Chinese were expected to advance was a vital part of the front line. All the time a steady column of

Bren Gun

refugees came southward along the road through the battalion positions. Fear of the Chinese had turned millions of feet in the direction of Pusan.

At this time, with a Chinese attack expected hourly, the situation was tense. Men slept with their fingers literally curled around the triggers of their rifles, or they did not sleep at all.

One evening, just before dark, Captain Mason made a routine inspection of the company positions. He found Woodbridge alert in his weapon-pit behind a loaded Bren-gun.

"Keep watching your front," said Mason brusquely. "There may be a show to-night, and I don't mean Rita Hayworth."

Mason was not particularly happy. These three weeks of retreat, of digging-in and pulling-out, had strained his nerves. Now they were to make a stand, here in the open, without so much as a blade of grass for cover. He had not slept for over an hour during each of the last three nights. What an infernally inhospitable country this was! For the first time he had begun to think back with longing towards the lazy, tennis-court-and-cocktail-party sort of existence he had known when he was newly commissioned just previous to the war. And now this lot had turned up. Angrily, with a sense of guilt, he tried to banish all such thoughts from his mind and concentrate on the job in hand.

"Keep an eye on the area to your right. The minefields will take care of anything trying to get through in the centre."

"Hi! Bloody hell! Look out! Hoy!" In an instant he became frantic; running forward, he shouted. "Stop! Don't move, you bloody half-wits! Mines! Mines! Corporal, for the love of Christ put a burst across 'em!"

Woodbridge carefully sighted the gun, and fired a long burst.

An old man, in the round black hat and flowing white robes of a village headman, a patriarch, was walking slowly towards them across the minefield. A group of refugees stood clustered round the barbed wire at its farthest extreme.

As the bullets droned around his ankles the old man slipped and fell heavily on his hip. He rose quickly but unsteadily, and attempted to cover the distance back to the barbed wire at a shambling run. Before he had run a dozen steps there was a shattering explosion. The small group of refugees, as if by instinct, threw themselves prostrate as the earth trembled beneath them.

Small stones and fragments of earth pattered to the ground. The patriarch had received the full blast of the explosion, and the splinters had transformed his living, breathing body to a shapeless, tattered corpse.

Mason was furious. He was purple with anger. "Blast!" he muttered through clenched teeth. "Blast the refugees! Damned nuisance!"

Woodbridge looked pensively at his smoking machine-gun. "Pity the poor old boy couldn't understand English," he said. "Otherwise he might have had a chance."

"Waste of a bloody good mine!" said Mason. He would not be conciliated until the dazed refugees, now without leadership, had been escorted through the battalion lines.

From a military point of view the tragic hordes of refugees presented an urgent problem. From the start of the conflict Communist forces had used this method of infiltrating behind the Allied lines to form guerrilla bands, or to blow up ammunition-dumps and communications. It was difficult, if not impossible, to know the difference between a North or a South Korean, and many of the refugees actually started from north of the 38th Parallel. Their numbers were so great that it was impossible to search each one for arms or demolition materials.

One aged woman was found to be carrying a grenade fastened into a tight bun in her hair. The Chinese, she explained to her interrogators, had told her to deliver it to one Mr Kim in Suwon, who would reward her with rice for the journey to Pusan.

Visitors to Mr Kim found him sitting on top of a sizable armoury.

There was little the U.N. forces could do to ease the suffering of the refugees, of whom an estimated fifty-five thousand died during the first winter of the campaign. Occasionally there were opportunities; Parkington, early in the campaign, observed a massive Turk fording a long column of refugees on his back across a wide stream where the bridge had been destroyed, like an up-to-date St Christopher. The plaintive cries of the hungry for food never went unheeded. Often the troops themselves went short of rations.

At Pyongtaek Hurst, searching for a comfortable billet, broke into a barn which had been battened up with boards. It proved to be stacked with sacks of rice. He reported to Major Hickson, who decided to distribute it on the spot.

The news spread quickly. The barn was besieged by refugees, who suddenly materialized from all quarters. Hurst formed them into a queue. They were given as much rice as they could carry.

VIII

PROBING

It was at Pyongtaek that Lane acquired a houseboy. He was mounting guard one night at the end of a line of ruined buildings. It was a late turn, the last stag before daybreak, and before going off he was waiting for the first dawn light to creep over the horizon. The moon had long since retired, and it was quite dark. Behind him, glowing with a strange luminosity, was a heap of cocoons.

A silk farm had once flourished here. It had been destroyed, and the owners had fled, leaving the cocoons piled into one great heap. The penetrating cold had already killed the grubs which had been developing inside.

During his spell of duty Lane had often been conscious of the eerie presence of the cocoons shimmering in the darkness with a faintly sinister, he thought, hostile aspect.... Now he was quite sure that the pile had heaved of its own volition. He glanced at it again. A number of husks at the top of the heap were trickling down to the bottom. The movement attracted his attention by contrast with the surroundings, where nothing moved as the greyness of the dawn began to seep across the sky from the east. There was no breath of wind.

The movement of the cocoons increased, and a great number cascaded downward from the top, until the whole heap was displaced and a small boy emerged from the bottom. The boy took a sharp look round him, and began turning over some of the cocoons between his fingers and shaking them. He raised one to his mouth, and began to tear at the tough fibres with his teeth until he had made a hole large enough to extract a small brown grub, which he swallowed greedily. Lane, watching this activity from behind a pillar of masonry, stepped out of hiding.

"Ida-wa," he shouted, beckoning.

The boy hesitated, then, seeming to sense that Lane was disposed to be friendly, he approached, grinning the mechanical grin of the Korean. He was remarkably thin and wizened. His clothing was a filthy, torn shred of overall, and his age—it might have been anything from ten to sixteen years.

"Chop-chop, hava-no?" inquired Lane, lapsing into the dialect which had been evolved as a sort of common currency in language. The boy shrugged his shoulders, which were partly exposed, revealing the gaunt angle of his collar-bone pressing tight against the skin.

"Hava-no! This same-same chop-chop." He showed a handful of cocoons.

Lane shuddered.

"Where you live? You mama-san hava-yes?"

"Hava-no!" said the thin, piping voice. He shot

a downward glance at bare feet, spreading his scarecrow's arms in a gesture of finality. "Finish, mamasan, papa-san."

"You'd better come with me, then. Ida-wa!" The boy followed him eagerly towards the shack which Lane shared with Hurst and Allen.

When they arrived Lane went in and emerged with several tins of combat rations which Hurst had 'made' from an American truck-driver of his acquaintance.

Afterwards the boy stayed in the vicinity of the shack all day, offering to do small duties such as fetching water for the frequent brews of tea and wood for the fire, and washing out the mess-tins after meals. He exhibited a little school English, such as "please," and "thank you very much," and "London is the capital of England," as well as a few terms he had picked up from passing Americans. He was intelligent, with the sharp wits of one to whom life is a severe battle for survival. After three days, when he continued to lurk around the platoon area, always at their beck and call, Hurst suggested, "Why not give the little beggar a permanent job and take him around with us?"

"That's a good idea," Allen agreed. "He seems quite honest. We could give him a scrub and fix him up with a cut-down battledress."

"Oi'll give 'ee a shout, then," said Lane. He leaned out of the doorway and shouted, "Ida-wa!" The boy appeared, grinning, almost immediately.

"What's thi' name?"

"Name?"

"Name!" shouted Hurst. "Look!" He jabbed a

finger at his own chest. "Me Kim," he announced. "Understand? Me Kim! You?" He pointed a finger inquiringly at the small, ragged figure of the boy, over whose face there spread the dawn of enlightenment.

"Me Chaw Song One!"

He said it with great emphasis and pride, as if it was the sort of name to be either treated with awe or paid for in blood.

"Well," said Hurst, unimpressed, "from now on you're Jacky. Got it? Jacky!"

"Ja-cky!"

"That's right. And you're the new house-boy, got it? Many-many work-oh, many-many chop-chop. No work-oh, you finish." Hurst callously drew his finger sharply across his throat and allowed his head to roll forward in a horrifying attitude of leering vacancy.

The boy nodded. "House-boy, okay," he said. "Okay-okay. Jacky."

"And what's my name?" asked Hurst threateningly.

"You name? Kim!"

"That's right. And don't you forget it!"

"What'll it be? I can offer you gin or Scotch, straight."

Parkington chose Scotch.

Gilmour poured the drink, raised his tumbler. "Here's to a funny war. With unpleasant complications," he added.

"Had a newspaper cutting the other day," Gilmour said absently, as if thinking aloud. "Big headlines. 'British troops in fighting retreat.' Does it make any sense at all?"

"After a time we'll have to stop somewhere," observed Parkington, "and really give them something to go to press about."

"If we don't arrive at Pusan first. Who the hell wants to hold on to this?"

"I sometimes wonder what the chaps really think about it themselves," said Parkington, reflecting. . . .

"It's a funny thing," Gilmour said, "but they seem to do better when they've got a grudge; a real one. They actually detest being here and having to risk their necks over a lot of gooks, and they're sick of being pushed around; so you can be sure that whoever really starts something is going to get a hiding—just because our boys are angry. I don't think they give a damn for the principles of the United Nations as such. It's getting down to the old idea of professional soldiering again," he added, "not that I know much about that, or that I'd ever have been a soldier at all, given the option."

Parkington lit another cigarette. He was smoking far more heavily these days than ever before; nerves, he supposed.

"It's a great profession," he remarked, blowing smoke luxuriously through his teeth and watching Gilmour's face for the sign of his reaction. "I'm just beginning to enjoy myself."

The eyes that faced him were humorous. "Well, go and make a name for yourself, Charlie-boy," Gilmour said. "As for me, I'm an amateur at this lark. But I will say it has its moments. Come on, let's finish up this bottle. We won't see another for a month."

*　　*　　*

Sloan also had recently drawn the monthly bottle of whisky which was allowed to each officer and senior N.C.O. In the privacy of his own hut he drew the bottle from its hiding-place and prepared to uncork it, when there was the sound of a jeep drawing up outside. Sloan hastily thrust the bottle back into hiding.

The blanket which covered the entrance to the room was thrust aside, and an American Negro clambered awkwardly through the narrow opening. He was the largest Negro Sloan had ever seen.

"Hiya, sarge," he said, by way of introduction, in a rasping bass voice. In a confidential whisper he added, "Say, you happen to know any guys who got any liquor to sell?" Stooping to avoid the low beams supporting the roof, he produced a thick wad of dollar-bills from an inside pocket.

Sloan shook his head firmly, his eyes resting for a moment on the bait. "Sorry. There's nobody around here got any liquor. It's all gone."

"Gee, that's rough," rasped the huge American. He took a long draw at a cheroot, which wilted visibly; then, with a confident flash of his eyes, he added, non-committally, "Y'see, sarge, we get kinda thirsty back there."

"Can't you get liquor from the canteen?" inquired Sloan.

"No-sir. They won't let us have the stuff. There's a federation of women back in the States who make a heck of a noise about liquor."

"Well, I'm sorry——" began Sloan.

"Look heah, sarge," the American broke in,

"Ah'm willin' to pay twenty-five bucks for a fifth of good whisky."

Sloan pondered, mentally converting the sum mentioned into sterling.

"How much did you say?"

"Ah said thirty bucks."

"Scotch?" suggested Sloan.

"Sure. Scotch whisky."

"It's a deal," Sloan said.

He produced the bottle, and looked at the label with a tinge of regret, thinking of the golden liquid unrolling its way like a carpet of velvet into an alien throat. He handed it over, picked up the roll of five-dollar bills.

The Negro fondled the bottle reverently. He could almost hide it in his elephantine hands.

"Mind if Ah take a small drop?"

"Go ahead." Sloan indicated the tumbler. The American carefully opened the bottle and filled the tumbler, which held a third of a pint. Sloan stared in frank admiration as the whole amount disappeared at one long draught, as if the glass had contained warm milk.

"Ah-um." It was an explosive gasp of satisfaction. "Ah sure needed that. Ain't you gonna have a glass?"

Sloan declined on principle.

"Yessir, that's the right stuff. You got any more?"

"That's all," Sloan said with genuine regret.

"If youse can get some more for the same price Ah'll be along in a few days from now."

"I'll see what I can do."

"See yuh." The great bulk of the Negro disappeared through the blanket.

The jeep roared away with a protesting of gears.

A week passed at Pyongtaek; a fortnight. Nothing happened. The Chinese were reported in Suwon, but they made no attempt to advance to contact.

The few patrols which were sent out to reconnoitre the Brigade front returned, having found nothing. Nothing, that is, except the dreary expanse of rising foothills and the desolate villages, now all but deserted, smelling of the dank, slightly rancid odour of earthy decay which came to be associated with all the towns and villages of the Korean scene.

Parkington, with a carrier-borne section of his own platoon, went out just after dawn on one occasion to reconnoitre one such village—a collection of twenty or so huts huddled inside the fold of a hill five miles to the north. They reached the village without incident, without, indeed, seeing so much as the stirring of a dead leaf, and Parkington led his section on a search of the buildings.

At first sight they seemed to be deserted; there was no sign of any recent human activity. The area of the village was bounded by a low wall of loose stones which had partially collapsed, and was littered with broken pottery and a variety of other rubbish.

Rubbish and refuse were strewn over the floors of the first few miserable dwellings which Parkington and his men examined, as if the rooms had been hurriedly ransacked.

In the fourth hovel they visited an old man with a deeply lined face and a grey wisp of beard sat on the floor, crosslegged, alone. He reacted to the instruction with a diffident grimace that was half a smile, with the sort of detachment cultivated by zoo animals, as if he expected such visitors, had perhaps had them before, and was past the stage of wondering what they were seeking.

All the other buildings that Parkington searched were vacant, except for the last one.

Trying the door, he found it wedged tightly, but the rotten wood gave way before one assault of his shoulder.

At first glance the room appeared empty, but as his eyes became accustomed to the gloom—there were no windows—he observed that not five yards away a woman was hunched in a sitting posture in the corner of the room, which was quite bare of furniture.

As the daylight filtered in from the doorway she raised her head slowly. She was dressed in a brightly coloured kimono—her traditional costume. She was quite young.

The light which revealed the detail and pattern of her dress also exposed to view the burden which she clutched tightly, close to her breast; it was a dead child, quite naked. The feet and hands were a dark mottled blue; that much Parkington could see, and in a sort of horrified fascination, as she raised her head to the light, he knew that she had crossed the border-line of sanity.

It was her eyes that rooted his attention. They shone with a brilliant lustre from the dark, sunken depths of their sockets, under the tortured lumps of matted hair which fringed her forehead.

A sound came from her lips which was the crooning gibberish of a soul in torment. She made no esture of recognition of the presence of other human beings.

From the appalling sight of this unfortunate young mad creature Parkington turned his head and motioned to the others to leave. They went out, soberly fastening the door into its place. Shortly afterwards they started back to the battalion positions.

"How long will she live?" The question revolved in Parkington's brain with sickening repetition on the journey back.

He hoped it would not be for long. . . .

Several days later a patrol captured two Chinese soldiers. They had been lying in observation, unobserved, on a small hillock a mile from the forward positions, for a week, until the cold had defeated them, and they had crawled out of hiding on limbs virtually useless from frostbite, to give themselves up.

And now, becoming bolder from the lack of any activity on the part of the enemy, strong detachments of U.S. Regimental Combat teams, units of Brigade strength, began to probe forward on the British sector along the main supply route, supported by the large Patton tanks, fanning out over the plain in the region of Osan-ni.

All at once it did not seem that Pusan would be the limit of the retreat, after all.

IX

RAIN

From the first days of the concentrated offensive of the Chinese armies which had been gathering behind the security of the Manchurian border the tragic retreat of the outnumbered U.N. Forces from North Korea had continued with only slight resistance until the battle-line had fallen back into South Korea, well below Seoul.

It was at this time that the sudden death of General Walker in a road accident brought a new Field Commander in the person of General Ridgway, to coincide with a stiffening of resistance all along the line. The Allied defences, which at one time seemed likely to be driven back once more to the notorious bulge of the Naktong river, were stabilized, and the advance waves of the invading Communists were checked and thrown back, while the full strength of both armies remained intact, and untested.

They were checked by 'meatgrinder' tactics. 'Meatgrinder' was a strategy opposed to the cut and thrust of the former campaign in Korea.

Earlier, when the U.N. armies had pushed forward, they had done so by strong thrusts along the supply routes with columns of tanks and infantry, carving the country into large segments of territory which had been by-passed.

The North Koreans had wilted and finally broken under the onslaught of the mobile columns rolling up-country along the few roads which converged upon Pyongyang. The towns fell, deserted of all enemy; but while the scattered remnants fell back larger pockets of resistance developed in the hills behind the fighting-line, in the wild and mountainous country of the east, in the Sibyon-ni area, and in the southwest.

There flourished fanatical bands of guerrillas who lived by day in the isolated villages, who by night plundered and wrecked and raided.

Ammunition trains were devastated by mines laid under the rails. Vehicles moving along roads in the rear areas were sniped at. Occasionally there would be a pitched battle, but not often, for the guerrillas preferred not to risk their strength against well-organized opposition.

Although, in time, the menace of the guerrillas was brought under control, the intervention of the Chinese posed a more difficult tactical question. The Chinese came across-country. They came through the valleys and through passes and over mountain-tracks, ignoring the towns and villages as bases, and the roads as supply routes.

They employed few vehicles in comparison with the U.N. forces. These would be too vulnerable to the squadrons of Sabres and Mustangs which roared unopposed, low over the twisting ribbons which were roads and river-beds thinly spread over the broad

North American P-51 "Mustang"

patchwork of paddy-fields and arid hill country of Korea.

The Chinese had resources and man-power sufficient to cut off and destroy columns of tanks and infantry without support; and, having no plains to work in, the tanks were powerless to operate on their own in the mountainous country which the Chinese chose as their battleground.

And so 'meatgrinder' was evolved.

It was simple.

All you had to do was to find out where the Chinese were established on a line of hills, and the infantry dug themselves in on a range opposite.

Guns and tanks were brought up.

On a certain date, when everybody was ready, you started.

You began with the long-range artillery from ten miles away enveloping the hills in tall columns of dust flung up by tons of high explosive, followed by the quicker shellbursts from the more accurate lighter guns, at a shorter range. You bombarded the positions further with tank guns, while swooping aircraft plastered them with napalm and rockets, and the infantrymen, secure in their foxholes, let loose a murderous hail of staccato fire with rifles, machine-guns, and mortars.

This lasted for the morning. In the afternoon the infantrymen crept up the slopes of the hills to find out if anyone was left there. . . .

This was called 'meatgrinder.'

The Chinese, after a while, complicated the issue by digging their positions on the reverse slopes of the hills.

While the British held the line at Pyongtaek the skirmishing American patrols penetrated to Suwon and found it virtually unoccupied. It was doubtful whether the Chinese had held it in force at all. The U.S. troops overcame this doubt by indulging their natural flair for bravado, and erected a notice at the gates of the town which advised all entrants who were ill-informed on such matters that they were "now entering Suwon by courtesy of the —— Combat Team of the United States Army."

A similar notice-board erected near a small wooden bridge over a long-dried-up stream crossing the road declared that a certain section of an Engineer Company had constructed the bridge in the first place, blown it up in the moustaches of the enemy, and had repaired it again with staggering speed immediately the enemy had retired.

The publicity-consciousness of the Americans showed itself in other ways. Jeeps were stencilled with names in glaring white letters, artfully contrived: startling legends such as "Hell's Angel" or "Jungle Boogie," as well as feminine names which ran the gamut from Chloe to Margie.

With Suwon secured, the battalion moved from the position of Pyongtaek, and advanced several miles to Osan-ni, where it stayed for a week, as corps reserve.

The village straggled away from the road to Suwon, meeting a low ridge of hills at its extremity. A few weeks previously a number of Chinese troops had been observed moving among the buildings by spotting-planes. An air strike had been called down which effectively transformed the majority of the dwellings into uninhabitable wreckage. The Chinese by this time had left. The only casualties were among the handful of peasants who still lived in the village. The advancing Allied troops found them, days afterwards, among the rubble; the dead, and those who wished only for the release of death, with limbs burned or shattered, and faces twisted in grimaces of pain and mourning.

In the centre of a wide circle of ruin a gruesome wooden image stood under a thatched shelter. Evil spirits more potent than its influence was able to counter had left it unscathed.

It was not long before the battalion was settling in once again among the uninviting accommodation which still remained.

The cookhouses, as always, were allotted the first choice of site, and they were quickly established, ready to produce the daily offering, with its

accompaniment of scalding tea. In the same locality
the men were choosing their own billets among the
ruined hovels and boarding them up as best they
could, a familiar practice which was always carried on
with a good deal of banter.

"Where are you kipping, Lofty?"

"I've got a shelf, mate. I'm the only one on it.
You fixed up?"

"You wouldn't chuckle. I've only got lodgers,
that's all."

"What sort?"

"Family of three in the next room. Don't think
much of the old woman, but the little girl is a
smasher. I'm keeping 'em on at a reduced rent . . . they
do my washing."

A good deal of the tension subsided. It was no
longer necessary, for the time being, to live in constant expectation of an attack, to spend sleepless
nights staring into the darkness, and sleeping fitfully,
when it was your turn to sleep, fully clothed, and
with an uneasy consciousness of wondering what was
going to happen to-morrow, or the next day.

Somebody produced an old football, which was
punted about on a piece of level ground for long
hours. For the first time baths were improvised out
of petrol-drums. Mail was delivered by the Field
Post Office, and it was avidly read and answered.

Bundles of dated periodicals and newspapers a
fortnight old were received and distributed.

To Parkington and Gilmour, poring over a pile of
magazines inside the flimsy walls of an isolated hut,
it seemed that certain facets of ordinary society which

they had once taken for granted and now sadly missed were tantalizingly brought to their notice.

They were engrossed and silent for more than an hour, until Gilmour broke the spell on their enchantment by saying, "Come and look at this," in a tone of something like rapture.

Parkington looked. He saw the pages of a glossy society weekly spread on Gilmour's knees. There was a full-page photograph of an elderly group in evening dress, identified by the captain underneath.

"Somebody you know?"

"Never seen 'em before in my life. But just look at 'em. Sir Geoffrey Somebody and his lady with Rear-Admiral and Mrs the Honourable So-and-so at the Hunt Ball. Don't you think they're superb?"

"I don't follow," confessed a puzzled Parkington.

"Well, just think of them," urged Gilmour explanatorily. "Think of them ten thousand miles away. What are they doing now? Sir Geoffrey will be out riding round his diminishing acres, talking about the Russians and the price of cattle feeding-stuffs to one of his tenants, I dare say, and the Admiral lounging in his club in Pall Mall, warm as toast, with the *Financial Times* and a fist round a glass of brandy."

"And the best of luck to them," Parkington observed laconically.

"I agree. But don't you see how well they represent everything solid and dependable about the old country, everything worth going back to?"

"I see what you mean, but what about this?" Parkington, grinning, held up the voluptuous portrait of a full-bosomed film actress in popularity-seeking négligé.

"There's a time for everything," commented Gilmour, with mock severity. "Anyway, I was just coming to that."

At an informal O-group, the next day, Major Hickson was more than usually jovial. He was a small, neat man with a crisp manner and a D.S.O. He had the uncanny ability to bridge successfully the abyss between rigid discipline and understanding of human frailty, which is a form of enlightenment known to few.

Occasionally angry, he was never known to lose control of his emotions.

He began with an air of mystery, with a dark glance round the circle of officers.

"There's nothing laid on for the afternoon, gentlemen, so the Colonel has suggested that we all go for a sightseeing tour. Any guesses?" he added provocatively.

"The Zoological Gardens?" asked Mason, catching the general spirit of facetiousness.

"The local Highlands, sir?" suggested Parkington, more practically.

Mr Pugh, commanding the third platoon of the company, offered hopefully, "Are we going to recce a port for disembarkation?"

"Sorry to dash your hopes, Peter."

Hickson carefully selected one from a packet of Lucky Strike and lit it with a precise flick of his lighter. He performed all his actions with infinite precision; everything was a rite.

"No. Let me tell you the whole story. The Turks encountered a spot of bother recently not far from here. It appears that they were surprised by a battalion of Chinese. When they had got over the first impact of the attack they put in a counter at bayonet level and re-occupied the position. They've moved forward now, and yesterday I took a walk over the scene with the Colonel, and he was so impressed that he suggested we all ought to have a walk round and observe the results, for the benefit of our morale. We start at fourteen hundred hours. Understood?"

"Roger, sir," affirmed Gilmour on behalf of his contemporaries.

The scene, when the company arrived, was set on a plain rising towards a ridge of hills. Here were the familiar scars on the landscape of multiple fortifications, where a defence line had been dug. The enemy dead were everywhere in a variety of recumbent positions.

The men, slightly awed in the presence of such carnage, fanned out across the plain.

Woodbridge, accompanied by Lane, studied for several moments the features of one of the dead, which were set rigidly in an expression of mirth; the lips curled back over the teeth, eyes puckered and half-open. The sub-zero temperature had preserved each of the corpses, but death had drained all colour from their features. They were like waxen images.

Lane said, "Looks loike they'm comin' aloive again any minute."

"Not this one." Woodbridge pointed to a jagged rent in the side of a bloodstained tunic where a bayonet had penetrated.

"Hope Oi never 'as to get that close," Lane said with a slight shudder. They moved on.

The bodies were thickest among the foxholes and trenches where they had been surprised and trapped by the sudden fury of the Turks. On the features of most Woodbridge observed a curious blend of babyish innocence and dispassionate bestiality.

They were quite young, the majority, and, strangely, a sprinkling of the quite old, with the crow's-feet of more than middle age wrinkling the corners of their eyes.

The company marched back to their lines in a more subdued state of mind; each man was thinking. Sooner or later we will come to this. We, ourselves.

There was a gradual lessening, for a day, of the cold, hard grip of the frost; then the rain came.

No clouds were visible. it was simply a scarcely perceptible darkening in the coloration of the sky, changing its familiar eggshell-like quality of hardness and brightness to a heavier greyness, like molten graphite.

The rain fell vertically, for there was no ruffle of wind, and it began sporadically in a light battery of large drops, increasing steadily in volume, drumming upon the tin roofs of the bivouacs and seeping into the ragged thatched roofs of the houses.

There was an outburst of inspired energy among the battalion lines in an effort to drag everything which was not waterproof under cover.

It rained all the harder.

This was no storm. There was no lightning, no

thunder, no hail, it rained as if it simply intended to rain, and there was to be no nonsense about it.

Rain like hard, leaden pellets beat up little dust-spots on the ground in the area around the dwellings where the dust had settled in long furrows during the dry months of the freezing winter. Rain lashed the low-lying rice-fields into pools of stagnant ooze. Sheets of metallic rain blotted out the sky and enveloped the surrounding area in a grey haze.

Rivulets of water impelled by gravity sneaked across the low ground to form swelling puddles among the dwellings huddled about the centre of the delta in which the village lay.

The first drops of water squeezed through the inadequate roof of the hut shared by Parkington and Gilmour in a dozen places, and began to patter dismally on to the mud floor.

Hurst and Lane had dug a narrow trench around their canvas-constructed bivouac, but this was soon filled, and the overflow covered the sunken floor in a thin, rising sheet of water.

"Water, water, everywhere," Hurst quoted bitterly, as he tried vainly to find a dry niche for his sleeping-bag, "not a bloody drop to drink."

The rain continued to fall.

The dried-up bed of the stream which struggled down, for no particular reason, into Osan-ni from the hills to the east, was transformed into a plunging, foaming torrent carrying with it fragments of brushwood torn from its banks on the journey downstream.

The puddles flowed into each other to form an expanding pool which began to encroach upon the lower buildings and lap against their raised doorways.

Forlorn articles of flotsam—old newspapers, pieces of box-wood, empty ration-tins, cigarette packets—floated about in the centre of the pool, and were lashed by rain. A clothesline, laden with sodden articles of clothing, broke under the added weight, and the garments were hurled into a pool of filth.

Still it rained.

With a resounding crackle of splintering supports a bivouac, insecurely constructed, collapsed, and the occupants emerged cursing fluently from the wreckage and made for the doubtful shelter of a neighbouring building.

Hurst and Lane, ankle-deep in swirling muddy water, with their belongings bundled on top of a platform of ration-boxes and protected by a ground-sheet, anxiously regarded the canvas roof of their dwelling, which had sagged under the weight of water on top, and now loomed over them, a vast threatening belly out of which water wriggled through in a rapid succession of pearly drops.

"Might be worse," muttered Lane through pursed lips. "Leastways, us can both swim. . . ."

The pool in the centre had now achieved lake-like proportions, flooding most of the low-lying buildings. It hardly mattered, now. There was nothing anybody could do.

Towards evening the rain ceased suddenly, as if it had been switched off. The sky remained grey, uncompromising, but it did not rain again. The battalion spent a night cloaked in misery, with a few exceptions, like Cave, whose billet was between two

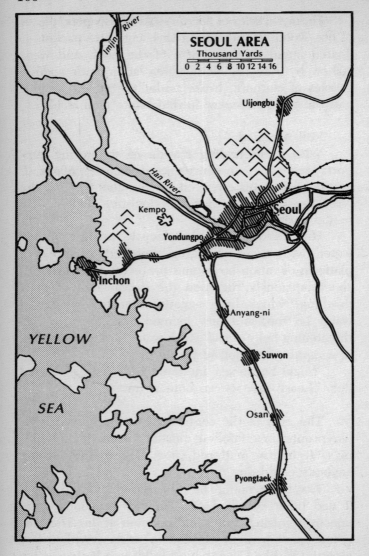

SEOUL AREA
Thousand Yards
0 2 4 6 8 10 12 14 16

Imjin River

Han River

Uijongbu

Kempo

Seoul

Yondungpo

Inchon

Anyang-ni

Suwon

YELLOW

Osan

SEA

Pyongtaek

large shelves in a deserted annexe. It was not ideally comfortable; there was not much room. During the preceding nights Cave had distinctly heard rodent teeth crunching a piece of biscuit in the corner. But during the rain he lay on top of his sleeping-bag listening to the discordant sounds of hissing and dripping and pattering from the security of his impenetrable shelter.

In the morning it was bitterly cold, with a rising wind. There was a thin coating of ice on the sheet of water, which had receded noticeably.

The process of restitution began.

X

THE ROAD BACK

In its earlier stages the war in Korea was a fluid war. A war of continual advance and retreat, where none of the fighting was static and no fighting unit could depend on remaining for more than a few days in the same spot. The command "Pack!" became commonplace in the Korean vocabulary.

After a week at Osan the Gloucesters packed up again, and their lorries rumbled north to Suwon, where they veered east towards Ichon, on the central sector, to leaguer among the hills of Pabalmak, a few miles to the south of the sweeping arm of the Han.

The area of Pabalmak was a series of towering heights upon which the Chinese had established themselves and dug a line of defence. Facing them, the U.S. 1st Cavalry Division had been given the task of dislodging all enemy south of the river.

The British 29th Brigade were committed to assist in this undertaking. And during the third week in February the Gloucester battalion were fully in action for the first time in the campaign.

* * *

The battalion's transport approached the area along a narrow road on which engineers were still working to shore up the banks. It was obvious that this was a fighting zone. Every few moments artillery thundered from positions near the road. There was the occasional chatter of machine-guns in the hills. American jeeps and supply lorries, and tanks with their noses garishly painted in stripes to resemble the head of a snarling tiger, choked the road which led to the rear supply bases. This road ran for some miles parallel to a river-bed, in which several enemy dead were lying face-downward on the lower slopes.

Across a small plateau flanking the hills where the road twisted past a skirmish had taken place a few days previously, and a greater number of Chinese dead were to be seen. One lay slumped across the lip of a dugout cunningly woven into the background of shrubbery, so that only a narrow slit showed. His cheek was laid along the butt of a machine-gun, and his fingers were curled around the trigger-grip. The other hand was employed in clutching a grenade, and he had been killed in the moment of taking out the pin with his teeth.

The battalion took up positions on three adjoining heights, and immediately began to dig positions.

Parkington's platoon area was located on the top slopes of a hill flanking the battalion position in the centre of a large saddle of high ground which overlooked a range of mountainous country stretching miles to the north, where the Han river occasionally sparkled through the haze of distance.

The hill itself was thigh-deep in coarse scrub and small, wiry thorn-bushes which tore at the uniforms of the troops as they climbed to the summit, where the weapon-pits were dug in the sand-and-rock surface. Soon the Korean porters attached to the battalion were labouring and sweating towards the hill-tops with boxes of rations and ammunition strapped to the Everest-packs which were fastened to their shoulders.

In six hours the battalion was firmly entrenched, facing the Chinese. Sloan, going on a round of the trenches, said, "Don't make too much noise, and don't light any fires, and don't walk about on the skyline. And if you see anything moving about in front after dark shoot first, and we'll hold the inquest in the morning."

There were murmurs of assent.

The nearer hills, peopled by the Chinese Communist forces, showed no activity, brooding sombrely, silent. The note of entrenching tools striking against rock had a cheerful ring.

The artillery had ceased. Only the distant echo of an occasional isolated shot sometimes carried over the hills, merging with the protesting of tracks and the muffled beat of powerful engines as a squadron of Patton tanks maneuvered in the valley.

When dusk fell the men, heavily muffled against the cold, slipped into their dugouts.

The moon rose in a clear sky.

The moon was bright and full, and it illuminated the hills in such a way that they seemed to glow with a strange phosphorescence of their own, against the

Patton Tank

horizon. The narrow re-entrant which Woodbridge's section looked down into and guarded was invested with a ghostly ethereal light which etched its detail in black and silver; the black of the thin tree-trunks of a grove of firs half-way to the valley below, and of the shadows, and the silver of the undergrowth silhouetted against the dark mass of the huge mound of the opposite hill. The night was still apart from a faint rustling of wind, and the periodical bark of a mortar as a flare was hurled across the valleys to become a brilliant pendant against the dark bosom of obscurity.

Just before midnight the sound of shots came from the American sector, but in ten minutes silence was restored. There was a long pause, punctuated by hushed conversation between the slit-trenches occupied by the men keeping watch. All at once there came a series of short machine-gun bursts, followed by a volley of rifle-shots from close at hand; Mr Pugh's platoon, which was situated on the left and slightly to the rear of the company position, had opened up.

Woodbridge, from his position in the centre of his section's weapon-pits, said in a subdued voice, "Watch your front. They may be coming this way."

A quarter of an hour crawled by.

From the grove the faint crackle of a breaking twig, which could easily have been a magpie. . . .

A shout, carrying over from a long distance off. . . .

The slight drone of an aircraft passing over at a great height. . . .

Lane, leaning against the butt of his Bren gun, was watching intently the slow-moving shadows among the firs as a trio of flares burst simultaneously a mile to the north.

The shadows seemed to fade at irregular intervals towards the edge of the trees, and flatten into the ground. Lane rubbed his eyes hard, and stared again. Nothing moved.

He nudged Woodbridge, pointing.

"Somethin' down yonder."

Woodbridge peered over the parapet of the trench. At first he saw nothing, until a series of dark patches moved across a gap in the undergrowth, four hundred yards down the hillside.

In a hoarse undertone Woodbridge said, "They're coming up along the track. About ten of them. They'll pass right in front of us. Get them in your sight, but don't fire until the Bren opens up. Don't make a noise."

There was a steady rustling now in the bushes, and a scrabbling of loose earth.

Three hundred yards. . . .

The Chinese were just visible, moving slowly and doubled up, weaving in and out of the cover.

At two hundred Woodbridge noted twelve figures passing across his line of vision.

At one hundred the laboured breathing of the enemy patrol could be heard distinctly as they mounted up the narrow track which passed directly in front of the section positions.

Fifty yards. Thirty. Lane hunched his shoulder behind the gun, trembling with anticipation. The features of the Chinese were now clearly visible.

At fifteen yards Woodbridge tapped Lane's shoulder, and the night was suddenly hideous with the noise of gunfire.

Seven fell immediately under the withering blast of the Bren. Three more followed as the rifles picked them off. Of the remaining two, one raked the section with a burst from a carbine before slithering, mortally wounded into the brush.

The survivor panicked, crashing downhill through the scrub until a fusillade from all the section weapons poured into his retreating back. The crashing echoes ceased, making the silence more real.

There were no casualties in the section. A bullet had holed the magazine of the Bren, passing within an inch of Lane's head.

For the remainder of the night there was no peace, as if the encounter had been the signal for a general resumption of the fighting. The mortars began a general bombardment. The rattle of small-arms fire came from all quarters. The Chinese set up a machine-gun on a pimple of ground a mile away and fired spasmodic bursts into the battalion positions. Bullets whined and pinged among the rocks. Just before dawn the machine-gun was withdrawn.

It was not until morning that Woodbridge and his section were able to snatch some time for sleep. The incidents of the night had left them slightly exhilarated with their success, which was further enhanced when Major Hickson conveyed a signal to the platoon expressing his congratulations at the result of their first action.

All the same, some of the men turned in with uneasy consciences. Next time perhaps they would be the attackers. . . .

At midday the artillery recommenced their barrage.

From the top of the hill Parkington could see the bright orange flashes from the muzzles of the heavy American 115-mm. 'Persuader' battery, which were mounted along a row of poplars lining a river-bed several miles to the southwest. The flashes were followed at intervals of several seconds by the sound of the explosion of their delivery, and the shells passed overhead with a noise recalling to Parkington the rustle of autumn leaves among the beeches of a Buckinghamshire wood. And on the distant heights falling shells exploded in grey mushrooms of rising dust on the Chinese positions, and the dull, muffled boom echoed back.

North American F-86 "Sabre"

During the afternoon the curtain of artillery-fire was lifted to allow an air-strike to go in on a hill where an observer-plane, one of the shuttle-service of droning Harvards which slowly circled the area all day, had reported movement.

A squadron of Sabre jets moved in, flying high, at a great speed, like a shoal of predatory swordfish. They circled the hill once, in a sweeping orb, losing height. Peeling off, they swept into a vertical dive and dropped the containers of napalm which had nestled underneath the wings, like lice. The bursting napalm sent up volumes of oily smoke as the hillside ran with jellied fire. Swooping again, the jets poured rockets into the confusion they had created. The rockets streaked from the wing-tips with a puff of ignited gas and exploded, out of sight.

The jets too went out of the range of vision as they daringly levelled off at altitudes of a few feet below the contour of the hills. They attacked with cannon-fire, turning and twisting time after time above the hill to go once more into the attack, while a steady stream of machine-gun fire from the defenders rose from the beleaguered foxholes.

Parkington, watching the strike through binoculars, was to see many more air attacks during the campaign. It was a favourite softening-up process, beloved of the American military chiefs.

The advantage was always with the attackers. Only on one occasion did Parkington see a jet destroyed, when a Sabre, hit by machine-gun fire, burst into flames and hung crazily in the sky for several agonized seconds, stricken, trailing smoke, until it finally keeled over and went into a fatal, plunging dive. The pilot parachuted to earth, but long before he reached the ground his body was riddled by Chinese bullets.

By this time the Chinese had begun to strike back on the Allied hills with accurate mortar-fire which sent the men back into the shelter of their dugouts. A bomb fell on Battalion H.Q., wounding several. Another burst harmlessly in the centre of Gilmour's platoon area.

The battle was beginning to close.

*   *   *

On that night the Chinese heavily attacked the American hill. It was a surprise attack; fighting raged fiercely at close quarters. The Chinese always preferred to attack at night, lying low during the day. It reduced the odds against them, when the artillery was silent and the jets had returned to their bases.

Parkington's platoon saw the action as a series of brilliant, searing flashes mingled with the soaring lines of tracer bullets and the white glow of flares. The ground underfoot vibrated incessantly from a continuous succession of explosions. Powell, tuning in the receiver of his "88" set, listened to a garbled cross-current of signals being transmitted from the American sector, American voices...

"Haversack blue, we are running very short of ammunition; if you have any to spare..."

"...Goddam sons of bitches are running about on top..."

"Dovetail.... Come in Dovetail.... Come in!... Over!"

"...located two M.G.'s bearing two-two-seven, bearing two-two-seven..."

"...I am being attacked..."

"...For Chris' sake stop chucking those flares about—it's like daylight up here..."

"...Dovetail, are you there, Dovetail, come in, Dovetail..."

"...This is ten, this is ten, we are coming down, can you hear me?..."

"...Dovetail..."

*   *   *

By midnight the hill was in Chinese hands, and the Casualty Clearing Stations in the rear of the positions were overcrowded with G.I.'s, wounded and dying and dead, some crying out with the agony of their injuries, others stiffly silent, biting their pain back, waiting for the daylight and the helicopters which would ferry them back to the base hospitals.

An hour before dawn the 1st Cavalry regrouped and counter-attacked, storming the hill and fighting back every yard of the way to the top, where the enemy were now entrenched behind the added fire-power of captured machine-guns. After a brief, bitter struggle the hill was regained, and the depleted Chinese attacking force retired as the dawn rose and streamed back through the valley, passing across the front of C Company of the Gloucesters, who opened up a withering fire. The Chinese scattered for cover, leaving many more of their diminishing ranks dead among the foothills.

For the rest of the day there reigned an uneasy calm.

During the next three days the front was quiet, apart from the spasmodic exchange of mortar-fire, while the 1st Cavalry Division were relieved by the 25th Division, and the Allied forces prepared for the attack.

XI

HILL 327

The Communist forces entrenched opposite to the 29th Brigade, estimated to be in Brigade strength, were established on a range of hills which featured on the Intelligence maps as Bristol, Dursley, and Gloster.

The hill called Gloster, Hill 327, was the key.

It rose in a formidable ugly lump to a thousand feet, half a mile from the main battalion positions, covered with straggling firs, its surface corrugated into steep ridges.

It was decided by the High Command that a concerted attack would be made on the 16th of February by the British and American Brigades to dislodge the Chinese from their positions on the heights and force them back on the Han.

The Americans were to attack several high features to the east. The clearing of Bristol, Dursley, and Gloster fell to a battalion of the 29th Brigade.

The Gloucesters were selected.

Early on the 15th the battalion was briefed. Two companies were engaged upon the assault on 327. Hickson's company were to engage with a frontal assault while the platoons of Dog were entrusted with the task of ascending the hill in a diversionary movement, finally to swing to the left and attack Bristol.

Baker, following through, were committed to the attack on Dursley.

Preparations for the attack commenced on the preceding day as the American 'Persuaders' opened up with a first heavy salvo, and soon they were joined by the battery of 25-pounders leaguered to the rear of the battalion with rapid and accurate fire on Hill 327. The mortars of the 4.2 battery and of the battalion Support Company began to fire ranging shots on the hill-top, seeking out the enemy entrenchments on the reverse slopes.

"Everything all ready for the party, Charles?"

It was Major Hickson, visiting Parkington's platoon on the afternoon of the 15th.

"We're all ready, sir. Nothing to do but wait."

"That's the worst part," commented Hickson. His lined face seemed just a trifle older, Parkington thought, and it made you notice the greyness of the hair round the temples.

There was a pause in this brief exchange. Hickson was looking across the valley at the broad massif which dominated the battlefront, and Parkington followed his gaze, shivering slightly as a keen gust of piercing wind sighed in the firs, against the monotonous background of explosions.

"How are your chaps feeling about it?" Hickson asked quietly, turning his eyes towards the surrounding dugouts where the troops sat, cleaning guns, filling magazines.

"They seem quite cheerful; apart from Willis. I'm a bit worried about Willis, sir."

"Willis—eh! What's the matter with him?"

"I don't know, exactly. He looks rather ill. He won't say anything. I think it's just an attack of the jitters. He's over there." Hickson followed the direction of Parkington's nod, and saw Willis sitting at the edge of his dugout. He was a slightly built, very young-looking lad with a head of almost white hair, now overgrown to such an extent that it sprouted untidily over his ears. Normally fresh-complexioned, he seemed unnaturally pale. His face was expressionless, eyes staring forward, seeing nothing.

"He doesn't look too bright, does he? I'd better have a word with him. Send him along in about half an hour."

Major Hickson was alone in his dugout when Willis lowered himself into the entrance. For a moment or two he did not look up from the letter he was writing on a pad balanced on his knee, and when at last he did he appeared, for a fleeting second, to have forgotten about the interview.

"Ah—Willis! Sit down," he suggested, indicating an upturned ration-box. "I sent for you, didn't I?"

Willis sat down, and remained sitting in a rigid posture.

"You're not looking too well, Willis. Feeling ill?"

"No, sir. I'm all right."

"Well, you don't look all right. Something on your mind?"

"No, sir." Willis's eyes were sullen, his voice heavy with obstinacy.

"Have a cigarette?" Hickson passed over a packet.

"No, sir, thank you."

He lit one himself, letting the pause take its effect, and tried again.

"You're a regular, aren't you, Willis?"

"Yes, sir."

"You're married, I believe. Been married long?" It was a shot in the dark.

Willis was patently surprised by this shaft. His eyebrows rose sharply. "Just before we embarked, sir."

"I see."

Hickson let his eyes wander ruminatively up towards the latticed branches forming the ceiling of the dugout, drumming his fingers lightly against the side of a water-can on which he was sitting. He was thinking, "He's married already, and hardly looks old enough to be allowed out after midnight."

"How's your wife? Is she all right?"

"Yes, sir," Willis said doggedly. He paused before continuing, seeming engaged in a tight struggle to force the words out. "She's having——"

"A baby?" asked Hickson.

"Yes."

"Isn't that something to be pleased about?"

"Yes, sir, of course. It isn't that, sir. I've been thinking..."

"Sometimes," Hickson said vaguely, "we can think too much." He waited while the sound of scrambling footsteps passed over the entrance and fled away. "What is it you're thinking about?"

"It was something I saw, sir, in the last place—Osan. I keep seeing it again, in my mind."

"Go on, what was it?"

"It was a man, sir, but it didn't look like a man—that is——" Willis was talking eagerly now, almost with excitement. "It was like an animal, grovelling about for food in the rubble. You see, sir, he had no legs; so I thought..." His voice trailed away.

"Yes. You thought that there, but for the grace of God, you might go. And you don't want to go back to your wife and baby like that, is that it?"

"Yes, sir, more or less." Willis's voice was more subdued. "That's what I can't keep out of my mind."

"I see. And you're worried about to-morrow?"

"Yes."

"Sure you won't have that cigarette?"

"Thank you, sir." Willis took one.

"I understand how you feel," said Hickson, "because I'm rather nervous myself. But some of us have to be soldiers, just like others have to be miners and ballet-dancers, and this is the stickiest part, and there's no getting round it, so we'll have to finish it as quick as we can. There's a lot of chaps with us, you know; it's not an individual sort of business. The best player in a football side is no good without support, and our backs are pretty good performers." A triple salvo of crackling artillery-fire broke, giving emphasis to his meaning.

Hickson produced a bottle of whisky and poured out two glasses. "Before you go, get this inside you, and try to forget it. You'll be all right. Before we move off report here, and you can come up the hill behind me."

Willis drained the glass. The colour was ebbing back to his face. "Thank you, sir." He went out, saluting, into the daylight, with an air of semi-belief.

Mason came in with a roll of maps under his arm. Hickson, raising his glass, was aware of a slight tremor of his wrist.

"Bloody hell!" he exclaimed. "I've got the jitters now!"

There was a rime of frost round the moon that night, and the dawn broke through a sky pregnant with snow-clouds. A chilling wind blew across the valley and ushered in a fall of snow which descended quickly, alternating with frozen sleet. Towards midmorning the assault companies filed out of their positions and moved towards the start-line, a column of muffled forms in wind-proofs and cap-comforters.

From the hills to the rear echoed a deafening roar of artillery as the barrage recommenced, and the upper slopes of Hill 327 were obscured behind a grey mist of smoke and dust through which winked the scarlet flashes of bursting shells. The mortars joined with a hollow booming in their long barrels, their bombs scurrying through the air to fall out of sight, on the far side of the hill.

At ten o'clock the U.S. Brigade a mile to the east launched their assault. They were just visible from the battalion positions, minute helmeted figures streaming across a distant plain like a battalion of robots.

Half an hour later the Gloucesters moved in.

Their way led them along the bank of a small stream, across a footbridge, and over a quarter-mile of open country to the lower slopes of the hill.

Behind them, nestling between a cluster of dwellings called Pabalmak, were a squadron of Centurion tanks, mounting 20-pounder guns, and at frequent

4.2" Mortar

intervals among them Bofors guns had moved up during the night. The battery of 4.2 mortars were leaguered near to the stream.

Soon after the two companies had crossed the bridge and were fanning out across the intervening fields a jeep unloaded four Americans to join the group of Brigade Staff Officers watching the attack go in, from no safe distance. One was Ridgway.

Woodbridge, as he neared the hill, glanced sideways at his section, strung out at three-yard intervals, keeping a regular, steady pace, his mind attuned to the prevailing tension; the odd affinity of men exposed to a common peril.

And to Woodbridge it was a stronger affinity than he had imagined. He cast a reflecting thought back to his earlier, brief military training.

Strangely, he remembered little; it had passed by in a shadowy haze of drilling and running about and being shouted at by hard, not-rational, difficult-to-please fellows. In fact, nothing had seemed rational then, and he had puzzled about it in his logical mind, wondering why things were carried on in such a manner, so repugnant to his ordered mental faculties.

But no real impression was registered, could not be focused in his memory. Instead, of his former Army life, smaller impressions rose to the surface.

Of the atmosphere in a big London rail terminus in the small hours, returning after a week-end at home, when the great spaces were thinly peopled by uniformed figures, and others having the familiar lineaments of soldiers in civilian clothes. The station like a staring mausoleum, exuding ancient respectability, making you feel you had no business to be there, this time o' night; and the slatternly women in the mobile café handing weak coffee through a barrier of dirty crockery heaped any-side-up on the ledge;

saucers, slopping over, their rims laden with bits of sodden bun. . . . Climbing into the inside, like an intestine, of the last camp train, into a lung-sick, foul-breathing sweatbox of stale beer, cigarette-smoke, last week's *Blighty*, a boots-on-seat, go-to-hell aspect of muttered imprecations, of smug, whispered stories of NAAFI* girls in the family way. . . .

This was Woodbridge's early militarism, and he had accepted it from his distance.

But it had nothing to do with this, now; nothing.

"After all," something in him said, "there is something common to all of us: it may be fear, but it holds us together while it lives, in circumstances like these."

The ground understood began to rise sharply as the company merged into the background of coarse bushes which sprouted more profusely than ever at the foot of the hill. The mile-long slope to the top loomed straight ahead. It was appallingly steep.

Woodbridge, like the other section leaders of the leading platoons, wore a white patch sewn to his back so that he could be seen by the observers directing the fire from the valley, as the platoon mounted steadily. As they ascended, the 'Persuaders' lifted their barrage, and the Centurions, the Bofors, and the 25-pounders took it up with a concentrated barrage creeping slowly to the summit in time with the leading company, two hundred yards ahead.

Parkington, leading his platoon cautiously through the fringe of a cluster of ragged fire, was thinking

---

*Navy, Army, Air Force Institute. British Forces equivalent of our Post Exchange.

also of his training days; his long and exhaustive training; schemes; night attacks. . . .

Fantasia versus Utopia.

How different it was!

Creeping up under cover of a hayrick one hazy August afternoon, he had once surprised another cadet belonging to a rival army lolling against a gate and had shot him with a blank from a pistol.

The 'enemy' had casually glanced round and 'shot' back.

"You've had it, old man," he had drawled, and Parkington, righteously indignant, had claimed, "But I shot you first."

"Perhaps you did, but you don't imagine I'm going to sit in the bloody hedge all afternoon and miss all the fun?"

Yes, it had been fun all right, but not real, any of it, not like this was real. . . .

As the trees ended he waved back the flank of the platoon and worked stealthily forward through the naked bushes, scanning the overgrown ridge which confronted him for the tell-tale signs of earthworks.

There was nothing; nothing but the coarse scrub and the whirling, stinging sleet.

Nothing occurred until the assault companies had mounted more than half-way to the summit, and the artillery were pounding the bunkers which lay hidden among the bushes and rocks around the crest.

Then, seemingly from nowhere, grenades tumbled among the leading platoons and a vicious crossfire from rifles and machine-guns swept the whole line of the advance. The platoons went to ground immediately, finding the nearest cover.

Three men of Hickson's company did not rise. Sergeant Webb, of Gilmour's platoon, encountered a machine-gun burst which sent a row of bullets through the stock of his rifle and blew three fingers from the hand that steadied it. Hickson, leading his company, was wounded shortly afterwards as he strove to seek out the enemy bunkers barring the passage to the top. A short burst of fire spun him round, and dropped him with his left arm numbed and useless.

Gilmour took over temporary command of the company. Parkington's platoon, strung out across a ridge, engaged a small cluster of bunkers from a hundred yards' range. The air was full of the drone and sigh of bullets and the singing of shrapnel from bursting grenades. The Commanding Officer, who directed the battle from the thick of it, called on Dog Company, now bearing farther left, to swing across to the right and make for the summit.

"Are you all right, sir?"

It was Willis, scrambling up behind Major Hickson, who was lying in the position where he had fallen, waiting for the stretcher-bearers.

"Ah, there you are, Willis," he said, with a cheerful gesture of his good arm. "Now, you see, I'm the one who is out of action, and you haven't got a scratch."

"Anything I can do, sir?" Willis said in a low tone.

"No, thank you, Willis. I'm quite comfortable. You'd better report back to Mr Parkington over on the right. I expect he'll be needing your help."

"Righto, sir." Willis crawled back. As he turned away his eyes filled with tears of emotion.

Sloan said, "If we could only get that bastard we could get right in amongst 'em." He was referring to the occupant of a slit trench ideally placed on the edge of a small spur near the crest of the hill, who consistently and methodically raked the company front with a hail of machine-gun bullets.

Parkington, who crouched next to him in the shelter of a low gully, nodded acquiescence.

"Shall we have a go at him?" suggested Sloan.

"Not from here. We wouldn't have a snowball-in-hell's chance. . . ."

As Parkington spoke the bushes rustled some way over to the left, and they watched three men of Dog Company crawl through, converging on the machine-gun post which was pinning down the attack, under cover of a projecting mound which ended thirty yards from the enemy position.

"We're too late, anyhow," Sloan grunted.

Parkington recognized a platoon commander from the other company in the lead.

"It's Mr Reece," he said.

Reece and his companions wriggled along on their bellies to the end of the mound, which at that point gave no more than a foot of cover.

Reece, with his arm curved in an arc, leaped upright and was instantly killed by a point-blank burst from the machine-gun. The grenade fell and exploded a few yards away, in front. Seconds after the corporal behind him was killed in a second attempt with a grenade.

The survivor, crouching behind his inadequate cover, waited for five patient minutes while the machine-gun stuttered fitfully. Then he stood up carefully and hurled his grenade in a high lob which sent it curling into the mouth of the enemy bunker.

XII

OUT OF THE LINE

In the valley the gun crews and the tank crews stood silently by their smoking weapons, waiting for news. They could do no more. For two hours a steady stream of shells had poured into the hill, falling with unerring accuracy into the Chinese bunkers, while the gunners toiled, sweating, stripped to their string vests, lashed by sleet, and the tapering guns of the tanks recoiled from round after round as the lash from their barrels brought down the loose ragged thatch of the near-by roofs and shook the buildings to their foundations.

But now close combat had been joined, and it was infantry against infantry to decide the issue; the simple issue of who would remain, that night, as occupants.

On the left-hand slopes of the hill the platoons of Dog Company progressed, creeping through the bracken towards the summit, storming the weapon-pits which still resisted.

Mason, meanwhile, had been summoned from the foot of the hill to take over the company from

Gilmour, and he arrived breathless, to find Parkington's platoon pinned down, while Pugh and Gilmour were moving slowly forward.

The first platoon of Dog mounted to the summit on the east side, and encountered fresh resistance from enemy dug in on the reverse slopes. There raged on the knife-edged crest of the hill a desperate struggle for supremacy.

It was Mason who injected fresh enthusiasm into the flagging will of the platoons in the centre, Mason, urging them forward with a furious example, singling out each foxhole for a hail of rifle-fire before eventually they were near enough to drop a grenade in upon the occupants who cowered inside; and somehow it was Mason who survived.

Parkington's platoon, with a final rush, gained the summit on the western edge and joined in the mêlée which raged for possession. Behind them followed the leading sections of Pugh's platoon, as Gilmour wiped out the last of the opposition on the lower slopes.

The Chinese occupying the foxholes on the reverse side leaped out and ran as the whole crest of the hill swarmed with men; as they fled for the valley they were shot down like deer into the shrubbery.

It was four hours since the assault companies had crossed the start-line.

Hill 327 was won.

Dog Company filed off along the narrow neck of land which stretched out to Bristol hill, their objective, which they occupied without a struggle. The slit-trenches yawned empty. The Chinese had fled across the valleys to the north, leaving the hillside littered with their equipment. Baker Company, quickly following through, reached the top of Dursley hill without incident, and occupied the deserted bunkers.

Two hours after the Chinese had been evicted Mason's platoon were digging in around the crest of Hill 327. Lane, searching among the abandoned bunkers for a comfortable place to bivouac, was about to descend into one when there was a movement inside; an arm appeared, a head followed, and a dazed Chinese dragged himself slowly into the light of day, while Lane hastily cocked his rifle. Inside the bunker was another, dead. A grenade had exploded inside, and the full force had been taken by his companion.

He was passed down the line to the foot of the hill to join the handful of prisoners who were herded together, Chinese and North Koreans, distinguished by their blue trousers, mute and trembling with apprehension at the prospect of the harrowing tortures which, according to their propaganda machine, lay in store for all Communist prisoners of the decadent Western Imperialists.

The American troops had successfully gained their objective, a series of hill features dominated by a central peak called "Cheltenham." The combined Allied armies now commanded positions overlooking a range of hills which extended along the south bank of the Han river. As night approached the snow ceased to fall, and darkness settled on the hills under a calm sky. The platoons settled watchfully into their hard-won positions, on guard against a possible counter-attack.

Parkington, trying to snatch a few hours of sleep, was assailed by strange depressions, wrestling with his physical desire for sleep. His platoon had escaped comparatively lightly. Tonbridge, a reservist, a big jovial fellow with a slow delivery of speech and a reputation for performing feats of strength—Tonbridge was dead.

A grenade, bursting at his feet, had transformed his powerful body into a ragged, formless mound of tattered cloth and blood and sinew. It was hard to believe, when you wanted so much to disbelieve it. Tonbridge, with his sudden rumble of deep laughter when nobody else was amused; Tonbridge pushing a carrier on its side for a bet and having to marshal the whole platoon to right it again; Tonbridge, with his mock-serious full-moon of a face, digging three trenches without a pause, with his great tensed muscles standing out on his arms like knots in mellowed teak . . .

Tonbridge, blown into mutilated obscurity; into unrecognizable little pieces scattered over the hill; and somebody would write to his widowed mother in Stroud in terms of "We regret that, during the course of. . ."

Sloan, with a small fragment of shrapnel in his shoulder, would be back in a week, and two other men who had suffered superficial injuries from bullets, they would be back.

And soon the whole business would start all over again, and somebody else would be Tonbridge. . . .

*   *   *

Centurian Tank

But for the time being it seemed that the Chinese had had enough. The night passed without incident, and on the following day the battalion consolidated its position by ranging over the surrounding area, finding no trace of the enemy; and Able Company, rolling along on the formidable Centurions down the road which veered west through the valleys, towards the Han, returned, caked in dust, with nothing to report.

Two days later the battalion moved forward to new positions four miles to the north, and Parkington, rounding a bend in the narrow road in his carrier, saw the muddy waters of the broad river swirling below. He recalled the incident of the refugee child at Seoul which haunted the memory of his last crossing of the river, during the retreat, and wondered vaguely how many corpses had bobbed in the river, and how many bones were hidden under its mud banks during the years of strife this unfriendly country had seen, since the hordes of Genghis Khan had first ravaged the sleeping villages.

While the battalion settled in to their new defensive positions the Royal Ulster Rifles moved up to clear the low hills flanking the river, and there followed a period of quiet, for the artillery were now silent except for an occasional salvo over the river, where the Chinese had retreated.

A week after the battle of Hill 327 the 29th Brigade were relieved by a brigade of the U.S. 25th Division, and the Gloucesters went once more into reserve, moving west through Suwon along the main supply route to Seoul, and settling among the familiar devastation of another village on the border of the road—the village of Anyang-ni.

Anyang-ni, before the destroying forces of war had eliminated its character, had been a large village with a railway station and a number of small factories at its northern end. A few of the buildings remained almost intact, and afforded the battalion reasonable shelter. Parkington and Gilmour shared the office of a bottling factory which boasted a swivel-chair and a large desk, and cupboards filled with index-cards and documents covered with spidery characters.

"I wonder what the income-tax people would give to have a look at this lot," murmured Gilmour, as he carried an armful outside and dumped them in the annexe, in order to make room for his personal effects.

Groping in the bottom of the largest cupboard, Parkington made a find: a rather archaic and dilapidated gramophone came to light, and underneath it he unearthed a heap of dust-covered records.

Eagerly they set it on the desk and wound up the spring. When Gilmour moved the starting-lever the turntable began to rotate slowly, gradually picking up speed with a sinister creaking.

Gilmour said, "Good-oh. It actually works. Now, what have we got in the way of music?"

"The labels are all in characters," Parkington announced, after wiping the dust from the records with his sleeve, "so it will have to be a surprise."

"Bet your life they're native," said Gilmour. "Sort of thing you hear in the streets in Singapore; that hideous caterwauling that passes for voice-control in the mystic East."

Parkington picked a needle out of a small cavity inside the box. "We'll soon know," he said. He put a record on the turntable.

For the first second or two the sound-box crackled and hissed over blank grooves, and then came the first faint tinkling notes of a piano. Gilmour listened attentively. "By Jove, Charlie-boy," he broke in half-way through the record, "it's one of the Beethoven bagatelles! I'd almost forgotten the thing.".

They listened until the last resonant phrase died away; and Gilmour selected another record. It was a Mozart quartet, performed, if you could discount the scratching and wheezing of the instrument, with impeccable grace.

"Wonderful!" was Gilmour's verdict. "Whoever saved up this little bunch had a reasonable taste, gook or no gook. What's next?"

It proved to be a Chopin recording—the Nocturne in E flat—which for Parkington touched unexpected depths of nostalgia, bringing old forgotten memories to the surface. In the rise and fall of the poignant melody of the Nocturne there was that which introduced into the atmosphere a trace of the grotesque, an echo of the dignity of the drawing-room filtering through into the world of senseless brutality to which Parkington had become accustomed during the previous months.

They exhausted the supply of records, which ranged from fragments of full symphonies to short pianoforte studies by classical composers, and Parkington replaced the gramophone in the cupboard.

Anyang-ni was the village of the forgotten children. . . .

Orphaned, or deserted by their parents, who had joined the column of refugees moving towards Pusan—a column which was now exhausting itself into a thin trickle—the children of Anyang-ni roamed the area in small bands, fending for themselves.

There were a small number of girls who survived, but their privations had left a terrible imprint of want on their wasted bodies, and they no longer had feminine attributes; but the majority were boys of ages from six to fifteen.

They were filthy, ragged children. They were starving, slowly. They had the lined faces of old men ludicrously affixed to the bodies of ailing infants. They ran barefoot among the freezing slush of the churned-up ground, and slept among the ruined buildings.

They could be heard shouting in their shrill, brittle children's voices for 'chop-chop' to the troops who settled in the area, or to the drivers of trucks which stopped for any reason on the main supply route which ran past the village.

Need supplied them with ample cunning. Their eyes could become unnaturally bright with impassioned pleading, or wrinkle into evil slits when they slipped like wraiths among the shadows at night, thieving and pillaging in and out of the buildings, while the occupants slept on in peaceful ignorance.

In the small ramshackle building where Hurst, Lane, and Cave lived Jacky the houseboy kept a constant vigil. He was now attired in a cut-down battledress, boots that were too large, and a beret that sat uncomfortably on his pear-shaped head. He was curiously aloof towards the children who roamed and robbed and begged. Although he did not treat them unkindly, remembering his own weeks of desolation to which he would one day return, there was in Jacky the lack of compassion for the less fortunate which is a trait peculiar to his race.

There was the occasion when Hurst and Cave made one of their frequent excursions in search of firewood for their billet. This time they went farther afield than usual, for the wreckage in the immediate vicinity had been stripped of all combustible material, so the two men crossed the railway-track and made for a little group of devastated hovels a hundred yards on the other side.

They had prised a number of slats of wood from the wreckage and were ready to leave when Cave saw, through a gaping hole in the wall, a small Korean boy running swiftly across the field, darting glances behind him, making for a small dwelling which stood on its own in the corner of the fields.

"Wonder where he's going?" muttered Cave.

"Never mind 'im," Hurst grunted. "Let's get back."

"Just a minute." Cave's eyes had caught the metallic glitter of an object in the boy's hand as he slipped round the corner of the building, and his rag of a shirt had seemed to bulge suspiciously. There had been a spate of losses from the billets of late.

"Let's go and take a dekko," Cave said. "P'raps the little beggar's got some sort of Aladdin's cave in that shack. Maybe we'll find Laney's fountain-pen and a few more items."

"Okay!" agreed Hurst. "We'll investigate the matter," he added pompously.

They walked across to the building, their footsteps crunching on the gravel of the yard outside. As they approached the door it was suddenly flung open, reeling crazily on a wire hinge, and the quarry flew out, evading Cave's grasp, and sped across to the shelter of the buildings they had just left.

"Nah let's have a look at the loot," said Hurst.

Inside it was dark, but a hole in the roof illuminated half of a large room, like a stable, littered with rice-straw, on which rested hundreds of empty ration-tins, pillaged from garbage-heaps. There was a heavy, sickly smell about the place which almost repelled them.

"Let's go," Hurst suggested pertinently.

But Cave had seen something stir under a mound of blankets in the corner. He went forward and lifted the corner of the top blanket, while his nose twitched with disgust as the smell increased in intensity. He jerked off the blanket.

Under it lay a boy of some twelve years, clad

only in a shirt. His face was bloodless and emaciated; a death-mask; but he was steadfastly licking out the inside of a ration-tin, and continued to do so, though blinking up at the sudden influx of light.

Cave's eyes followed the length of his thin, bare legs to the feet. One of them—the right foot, he noticed—was dyed a mottled black and purple, and the centre of it was open in a vivid crimson gash, oozing yellow pus.

At last the boy dropped the tin and began to shake with sobbing, tears coursing over the tight skin of his cheeks through tributaries in the dirt worn by many previous tears.

The two men made no comment, apart from Cave's sharp intake of breath. It was too appalling for words, and the reek of dead flesh was beginning to make them feel sick.

They made their way outside again and hurried back to the lines for a stretcher.

When they returned to carry the boy to the casualty reception centre a trio of others appeared, keeping a small distance apart. The departure of their companion broke through the hard protective barrier of their resistance. They stood round miserably in a small arc as he was loaded on, wailing in sympathy.

After a few days Sloan returned to the platoon. He did not return willingly. He had suggested to the M.O., who had taken a small sliver of shrapnel from his shoulder, that he was unfit, that he suffered from arthritis; that in any case he was too old, at forty, for "this kind of caper," and that he should be given a base job at Kure to make room for a younger man.

But the M.O., who was a very young man himself, had slapped him on the back and said, flippantly, "Cheer up, sarge; you're only as old as you feel, and if you're lucky you'll live to be a hundred. Anyway, you'll last for another six months."

And the next morning he had been put on a truck going north, and that was it.

He was not amused, and still less so when he was put in charge of the guard on his second night back.

And when, soon after dark, Battalion H.Q. sent a signal to say there were about sixty fires in his platoon area, and what the blankety-blank, it was a fuming Sloan who strode off in the direction of the trouble.

The fires, about a dozen of them, burned brightly around a large barn four hundred yards away, which had been occupied that day by a large force of Korean police.

The police, who performed various traffic duties on the main supply routes, and administered civil and security affairs behind the lines, were an organization well steeped in corruption.

Their pay was small, but their rice was adequate, and they were not above making up for the former deficiency by extortion from the refugees, amounting to naked robbery, and by a wide range of illicit deals in stores and equipment involving millions of inflated won. Behind their outward demeanour of fawning politesse many iniquities were perpetrated in the name of law, and their cloak of justice hid a dagger in its folds.

When Sloan reached the spot he found the police huddled round the fire in a tight circle, jabbering excitedly. There were one or two women in their midst. He stood at the fringe, rifle canted menacingly, and bawled, "Put these fires out, you shower of bastards. What d'you think it is, Guy Fawkes night?"

"No understand," said one.

In the firelight they peered up at him, bland smiles on their tolerant faces, and a cackle of voices broke out, which to Sloan said, "Who is this silly bloody Englishman, and what does he want?" To make his meaning clear Sloan pushed through the circle and began kicking the blazing fragments in all directions. There was considerable haste to rise among the Koreans, and a fresh outbreak of querulous voices.

Sloan passed along the line of fires, kicking at each. Returning, his anger somewhat abated, he glanced round and saw that the scattered wood had been patiently gathered in, and the fires blazed once more.

Walking back, Sloan stood once more at the edge of the circle of upturned faces. Overhead an aircraft droned, lazily, giving him an idea.

"Chinese!" he shouted, gesturing skyward. "Chinese planes!"

He ran five yards and rolled in the nearest ditch.

The police reacted with surprising vigour. There was an excited babble of voices. The fires were hastily stamped out. Three bodies pressed themselves down beside Sloan's into the soft mud.

XIII

AWAY FROM IT ALL

After a week at Anyang orders to move were received once more, and the Brigade leaguered in a reserve position not far from Ichon, towards the central front.

It was an area of gently undulating paddy-fields away from the supply routes where the war had passed by. Most of the villages in the district were occupied, and the peasants who lived in them worked all day in the fields, preparing the ground for the spring sowing.

Sloan said, as he watched a tent being pitched, "Everybody seems to have a tent, bar us. Where do they all come from?"

"Yanks, mostly," Hurst said succinctly; they were leaning against a low-built shed, the best accommodation on offer.

Sloan emptied his pipe against the wall. "You got anything to do right now, Hurst?"

"Nothing what can't be put off until to-morrow."

"What about Lane?"

"He's knockin' abaht somewhere."

"If I gave you a bottle of whisky and you took Lane for a ride in the fifteen-hundredweight..."

Hurst looked dubious. "They won't usually part for one," he said. "Two, maybe."

Sloan considered it. Two bottles meant sixty dollars.

"Two bottles."

Eventually he produced them, wrapped in a groundsheet.

Hurst tucked them under his arm and went away, whistling.

"Might try this'n," Lane said. "63rd Quartermaster Battalion." The words were painted in glowing detail on a brilliant red signboard, above a list of the places the 63rd had been, like an advertisement for railway travel in the Scottish Highlands.

Hurst swung the truck through imposing iron gates where an indifferent sentry stood stolidly chewing gum, without a flicker of interest as the truck swung into a courtyard flanked by tall brick buildings.

"Say," Hurst called to a corporal strolling towards a stores compound, "you guys got any tents?"

"Tents?" The corporal barely slackened his pace. Hurst might have been asking for a light for a cigarette. "See Cap'n Pinero, Supply Group Office."

"Where does 'e 'ang out?"

"Whassat?"

"Where?"

The corporal pointed towards a green-painted Nissen hut.

Hurst and Lane entered, carefully closing the door behind them. The captain sat in a canvas chair, a drab, precise little man wearing octagonal glasses. A printed card decorated his desk with his number, rank, and name. There were a dozen desks behind him in two rows, occupied by clerks, and a dozen typewriters clattered.

"What can we do for you boys?" It was a smooth, pleasant voice, tinged with a faint inflection of surprise.

It was Lane who put the bald question. It was Lane who carried the bottle. The neck of it stuck out of his trouser pocket and protruded just a little above the captain's desk.

"Tent?" The American looked apologetic; his voice sounded hurt. "Sorry, boys, no can do," he said. "I got three thousand on demand, but there just ain't one in the place, not even if you had a requisition."

"Thanks all the same," Hurst said abruptly. They went out.

Five miles farther along the route a U.S. Ordnance detachment were camped in a river-bed. As they lurched across the rough track leading to it Hurst said, "We'll try somethin' else this time. Let me have the bottle."

He stopped the vehicle in the centre of a circle of tents and approached a sergeant who had just emerged from the one in front. The bottle stuck out conspicuously from his lapels.

"Hi, sarge," he called breezily, "can you tell us how to get to Suwon from here?"

"Sure. Just turn around an' follow the..." The lazy voice petered out as the sergeant's eyes identified the label. "Say, buddy, that ain't a bottle of whisky you got there?" There was a quickening of interest in his tone.

"That's right. You say it's straight on down? About 'ow far?" countered Hurst.

"Whassat? About fifteen miles, I reckon. Mind if Ah jus' take a look at that bottle?"

"Go ahead." Hurst produced it, handed it over.

"Scotch!" The sergeant moistened his thin lips. "Oh, brother," he said, "Scotch!"

Hurst waited for a few seconds, then stretched out a hand.

"'Ave to be goin'."

The sergeant parted with the bottle with the enthusiasm of a beagle deprived of a fox it has chased through two counties. He hastily produced a wallet. "How much will you guys take for that bottle?" he demanded.

"Sorry," Hurst said shortly, departing. "We ain't thinkin' of sellin' it."

He climbed back into the truck and started the engine. The sergeant followed. He put his head inside the door and shouted, above the roar of the engine, "Ain't anythin' you guys want in exchange for that bottle of Scotch?"

Hurst switched off. "Can't think of anythin' offhand."

His entire attitude expressed the offhandedness of this deficiency of thought. "Can you think of anythin' we could do with, Laney?"

"No," Lane confessed, with a pretence of thinking deeply, "unless it's a tent. Us could do wi' a tent."

"Suppose it would be useful," admitted his companion. "Got any spare tents, sarge?"

The sergeant rubbed gnarled fingers over a balding patch on his scalp.

"Jeez!" he muttered. "We're kinda short on tents right now. What about a generator or a jeep engine? Or a coupla radio-sets?"

Lane was adamant.

"Wireless-sets doan' keep out rain," he pointed out.

The sergeant allowed not. He belched pensively.

"Sure. You wan' sump'n to live in, huh?"

"Reckon so, china," said Hurst, mixing his idioms with gay abandon.

"Like a tent, for instance."

"That's it."

"Listen," said the sergeant. "See that tent on the left." He pointed it out. "Wal, it's empty at the moment, but it's big enough to get your truck inside. Behind that one is another tent belonging to Lootenant Hoskin, who is in Inchon for the next few days. Me, ah'm on rotation to-morrow. So if you boys back your truck into that first tent we'll kinda borrow the lootenant's and put it in the back of your truck. An' if we're quick there ain't nobody gonna be the wiser."

The tent was dismantled and stowed away in ten hectic minutes. On the way back Lane asked, "What shall us do wi' the other bottle?"

"Celebrate," Hurst said.

The tent, when it had been erected, was large enough to accommodate six men, and it was occupied by Sloan and Woodbridge, and Hurst, Lane, Powell, and Allen.

Powell, who had a strong flair for improvisation, installed a stove of his own devising. It was of Japanese origin, salvaged from some convenient wreckage, and Powell had modified it as a petrol-burner, by attaching a feed-pipe to the top, which was also connected at the other end to a petrol-drum. Gravity forced the petrol through the pipe into the top of the stove, where it dripped through a nozzle into a flashpan at the base, and ignited. The flow was controlled by a tap in the pipe. The stove gave off a fierce, constant heat.

As Powell pointed out, there was only one fault. It was liable to explode at any moment.

It was an impressive device. The falling drops of petrol ignited with a sharp explosion, and, with the tap fully on, the stove vibrated with the pressure inside it, and gave out a throbbing roar, as if about to become airborne.

But in the evenings, when the stovepipe glowed with the redness of ripe cherries, and the light from a 12-volt bulb illuminated the tent with a soft radiance, the occupants of the tent enjoyed a measure of comfort which they had not known since the start of their Korean service. The prevailing question was still, "When are we going 'ome?" But with the men fully occupied during the day the time began to pass quickly.

For three weeks the Brigade rested. The Royal Engineers levelled a site near the road, and football-posts were erected.

For the first time officers and sergeants were
able to set up their own messes. American fresh
rations had replaced the 'compo' rations on which the
troops had survived during the last three months,
and now there were steaks and fresh vegetables to
take the place of the inevitable corned-beef-and-
dehydrated-potato hash.

Crates of Japanese beer arrived from the railhead, to be quickly consumed.

Without the persistent rumbling of artillery in
the background, far from the pitiless devastation of
the towns and villages on the main supply routes,
freed from the necessity of constant vigilance against
possible attack, the thoughts of the troops strayed
from the business of warfare, the war which was
raging thirty miles to the north, where a U.S. Division was preparing an assault on Seoul, having already outflanked the city by a drive along the coast
road, after retaking the battered port of Inchon.

The conversation in the messes turned to the
familiar cycle of reminiscences, other-world matters
which had no bearing on the present.

". . . we stopped at a little place called the Green
Man, just on the outskirts of the town. Quite accom-
modating, really, especially if you were there long
enough to get to know the barmaid, who was a bit
pregnant at the time, and the cider was enough
to . . ."

". . . old Marrow, that was 'is name, corporal, 'e
was then, '36, this was, mind, although I did 'ear 'e
got pensioned off as a sergeant-major at Bulford

about five years ago, an' I believe 'e got a job as a storeman in a cement factory after that, but, as I was sayin' . . ."

". . . an' I know it's official, because I 'ad it from the Brigadier's batman, bloke I was at school with in Bethnal Green."

"Chuck it, Cavey, for Christ's sake. You'll be tellin' us the Chinks 'ave all got yellow jaundice next."

As the month of March progressed preparations were made for the celebration of Back Badge Day, the Regiment's annual day of festivities, which falls on March the 21st, the anniversary of the battle of Alexandria, which won the right to wear a cap-badge 'fore and aft.'

A week beforehand the Royal Ulster Rifles held their own parade to commemorate St. Patrick's Day.

Their marched out of the their billets to the triumphant skirl of their pipes, and formed up for inspection on the football-field, under the slopes of the barren hills, with the kilted pipers presenting a colourful contrast to the drab backcloth of brown fields. Above the parade a trio of flags dipped in the light breeze, and the words of command sounded crisply in the morning air.

Only the shamrock was missing.

But the preparations for the 21st promised to introduce a number of features even more foreign to the Korean scene. A fête was to be held, with side-shows practising such activities as climbing a

greasy pole, kicking a football through a hoop, shooting for sweepstake prizes. The Pioneer section worked
on the construction of a huge effigy of a Chinese
soldier with a leering yellow face and a double row of
teeth which imparted a tombstone-like quality, being
fashioned from old, white-painted ration-tins, which
it was the business of the competitor to knock out
with hard wooden balls.

During the afternoon a football match had been
arranged.

A large delivery of turkeys from American sources
formed the nucleus of the extra-regimental dinner
which was laid on for the day. Beer in crates mounted outside the PRI tent.

The day promised fair. During the last week the
sun had broken through, shining from a clear sky. It
was a weak, wintry sun, detracting little from the
bite of the keen March winds which persisted, but it
was quite evident that the sun had time on its side.

Under its influence the countryside stirred to
the first influence of the coming spring, like a man
near to drowning who is revived by artificial respira-
tion, although as yet it had not begun to react visibly.
The magpies alone recognized the passing of the
winter through which they had clung to life when
most other birds had either migrated or perished.
They celebrated its dying throes with their fractious
and noisy courting among the branches of the poplars
lining the valley.

But by night the temperature still fell below
zero, and Cave, passing away the two hours of his
guard, harked back to the generous warmth of his

sleeping-bag, from which he had been parted with great reluctance in the early hours of the morning. Being relieved at last, he returned to the tent in which the other occupants were breathing heavily in the depths of sleep. It was half-past five.

With reveille at seven, it was hardly worth while turning in again. He would just sit in front of the fire and make a can of tea, and take it round when the other men woke up.

Cave switched on the petrol and heard it dripping into the flash-pan at the bottom of the stove. He felt exceptionally tired, and while he was fumbling in the darkness for a match his brain relapsed into drowsy unconsciousness, and his head slumped forward, and it was twenty minutes before he awoke, his hand clutching the matches in his pocket, rubbing his eyes, thinking, better get the fire going; nearly dozed right off there . . . Unfortunately it was too dark to notice the pool of petrol which had overflowed from the stove and was now seeping into the straw which covered the ground at his feet. Directly he struck a match the fumes ignited with a blast which knocked him backward from his seat, instantly wide awake, as the petrol caught among the straw. Vainly trying to smother the flames with a blanket, Cave shouted, "Fire!" at the top of his voice. Everybody woke up and struggled out of their sleeping-bags.

Sloan, who slept nearest the fire, was the first up, beating the flames with his bare hands, as they encroached upon his bed-space. Soon the others joined in, half-awake, stumbling about in the flickering light.

The tent filled rapidly with choking carbon-monoxide fumes. With a roar the petrol-tank was consumed by fire. It was the end.

Sloan gasped, "Get outside! Quick."

They groped towards the entrance, coughing out the strangling fumes from their lungs, their eyes moist and smarting, and tore desperately at the tent walls in an attempt to drag their belongings to safety, but the fierce heat drove them back. The roof of the tent was now a swirling maelstrom of fire.

Lane, who was last out of the tent, collapsed in the entrance, but he was dragged to safety, and quickly revived in the cool outside air.

There was a moment of bitter gloom as the tent collapsed entirely, and flames ravaged the wreckage from end to end.

Nobody reproached Cave. The catastrophe was too devastating for recriminations. While the flames died the piercing wind cut through their terribly scant underclothing, and they huddled closer to the centre, where the tent-poles were still giving out a cheerful blaze. Hurst found a supply of tea, milk, and sugar among the ashes, and began to boil a can of water on the blazing wood. There was nothing to be done until the morning.

Woodbridge, searching among the ruins of his belongings, found only one item which was un-damaged—a flimsy French magazine discarded by a Belgian, in which he had been translating for Hurst's benefit a lurid account of an alleged incident in the early life of Honoré de Balzac. It was Lane who discovered a smouldering fragment of canvas to which was attached the name of the tent-maker, and the claim that it was "proof against fire and water."

Hurst made the tea, and it was passed round the circle of men who crouched over the burning embers of their possessions, in the gloom of early morning, waiting for dawn.

XIV

TOKYO LEAVE

Late on the 20th came the order from Brigade Headquarters to move to a new location in the town of Yongdungpo.

At this period of conflict the changing fortunes of the U.N. Forces were entering a phase of prosperity, and the new 'meatgrinder' tactics had rolled the Chinese back across the whole breadth of the Korean peninsula. U.S. Patton tanks had roared in triumph through the newly liberated city of Seoul, to be welcomed by the handful of natives who remained, emerging from their battered hideouts with vacant faces to which the element of surprise was a stranger.

The enemy battalions were steadily driven back, contesting every yard, into the hill-region of Uijongbu.

On the central front the 27th British Brigade, with the French battalion, the Canadians, and other units which gave the effort a truly cosmopolitan flavour, had fought and won the fierce struggle which raged for the heights north of Wonju.

This success wiped out the Chinese threat to the centre, and provided Hurst with a new jest.

"Wonju?" he inquired cynically. "What's all this fuss over one bloody Jew?"

Early on the 21st of March, which was Back Badge Day, the battalion once more packed up, and its vehicles threaded their way out on to the main supply route, to head north for Yongdungpo. Before the last of the men had clambered into the carriers hordes of Korean villagers had gathered like buzzards around carrion, and were busy among the litter and garbage-heaps, probing every inch of the area where camp had recently been struck.

The celebrations were cancelled, the tents removed from the football-field, but the goalposts were left standing, soon to be dragged down and used as firewood by the first household to carry them off.

The effigy of the Chinese soldier was left, but the Koreans showed a strange deference towards it, keeping their distance. Perhaps in the simplicity of their souls the idea was evolved that it was a powerful juju of the Western world, and possibly it was allowed to rot in peace.

Yongdungpo is the sprawling industrial right hand of Seoul, lying five miles south of the capital across the Han river, but the heart of its industry no longer beats out the rhythm of production, because, like Wordsworth's London, "all that mighty heart is lying still."

It has been stilled by the weight of bombs, released from the bays of aircraft, by salvos of heavy artillery shells, and the dry-rot of indecisive war has settled over the factory chimneys which remain like fingers of scorn to point skyward over the dismal rubble.

The machines also are left; acres of machines, twisted and rusted relics of looms and lathes from which all shelter has been torn away, so that rain and dust alternately settle on the pedals and handwheels once worked by industrious hands and feet.

Strangely, as if by common accord between the occupying forces, the main brewery was unscathed, and under American direction continued to produce gallons of weak and tasteless beer, which was distributed to all troops settling in the area.

The Gloucesters settled on the northern fringe of the town, close to the Inchon road, the longest surfaced road in the country.

And now the town took on a new identity, for, protected by the barrier of the Han from a sudden offensive, and containing sufficient large buildings to house quantities of men, it swiftly became the main base for the Allied armies foraging ahead.

At the crossroads of the town centre there was a constant flow of vehicles to and from the front, and the roar of their engines was punctuated by the shrill whistle of the Korean policeman on point duty in the middle.

At various points among the remaining factory buildings the support units of differing nationalities were stationed—British, American, South Korean, Turkish, and Belgian detachments of engineers, workshops, transport and supply depots.

Soon after the arrival of the battalion in Yong-dungpo, by an odd stroke of chance, Hurst and

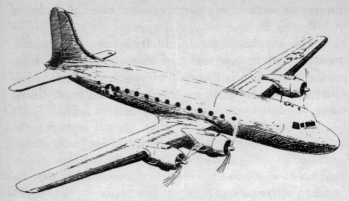

Douglas C-54 "Skymaster"

Woodbridge were drawn together for five days of leave in Tokyo.

As the time for their departure drew near both were excited at the prospect. Woodbridge because he had always had a secret curiosity towards the peculiar traits and culture of the Japanese as a whole, and Hurst because of a strong desire to investigate the geisha system. Moreover, for the first time in what seemed at least a decade they would be able to taste, for a short time, the delights of civilized comforts which a city modelled on Western standards could provide. On the morning of the journey they both rose before daylight, and after a quick breakfast joined the party of about a dozen men from the battalion who had been allocated leave by ballot.

At seven they were deposited by a lorry at Kimpo airfield, where other leave parties, largely American, were walking about aimlessly, waiting for instructions. Eventually they were detailed off in queues to settle down for the long wait for a plane.

It was an uncomfortable period. A bitter wind blew across the airfield, and the area where the queues waited was exceptionally muddy. At last, after three hours, a flight of four-engined Skymasters touched down on the field, and the queues filed into them. Hurst adjusted his safety-belt, struggled into his parachute harness, and, after a few secretive puffs at a forbidden cigarette, fell asleep. He had, as he confided to Woodbridge, "knocked abaht in these things before, many a time."

He was woken up four hours later, surprised to discover that the Skymaster was coming in to land on Tokyo's main airfield.

Coaches were waiting to transport the British troops to the Ebisu hotel, a leave hostel given over entirely to parties from Korea.

After a quick documentation at the hotel Hurst and Woodbridge were directed to their room—a spacious, centrally heated room containing two beds with clean white sheets and pillows.

Woodbridge did two things. Firstly, he drew a new uniform from the hotel stores, neatly pressed and tailored. Secondly, he made for the shower-baths and stood under the rose for an hour, steaming and utterly content as the clinging, cloying taint of Korean earthiness evaporated from his body.

Afterwards the new, glowing Woodbridge went downstairs to the cafeteria and enjoyed a dinner such as he seemed not to have enjoyed for years, served by pert Japanese waitresses with starch-fronted aprons. A small orchestra played subdued light music in a corner. The cafeteria was gay with flags and bunting, and the waitresses smiled and nodded at his bidding, as if in response to the quiet rhythm of the violins.

Having satisfied his appetite to the full, Woodbridge went to look for Hurst. One of the men in the room opposite said, "Your mucker went out about 'alf an hour ago, corp, after 'e got cleaned up. Left a message to say not to wait for 'im, because 'e might not be back 'til late."

Hurst didn't return at all that night.

The atmosphere in the Ginza beer-hall was pungent and acrid with cigar-smoke and uproarious with the noise of the troops who packed that establishment to suffocation.

Hurst sat at a table at one side of the hall, and next to him sat a man from another company named 'Splitpin' Edwards, whose nickname was derived from his thin, willowy frame and the fact that he was knock-kneed. Hurst had only a passing acquaintance with Edwards, but the two had reached the entrance to the Ginza simultaneously, and had gone in together and sat down at one of the few vacant tables.

"Not much cop, this place," Edwards said. "Too much bloody noise. You can't even hear yourself, let alone the band."

Hurst glanced around the hall, and noticed for the first time five bland little men in white dress suits with muted silver instruments who were striving to force the beat of their music through the hubbub of a myriad voices.

Voluptuous girls in short flared skirts and low-cut blouses served beer at a frantic speed, and found time to pose among groups of Servicemen for the small battery of commissioned camera-men who wandered from table to table.

The beer-hall contained a cross-section of all the nationalities serving in Korea who had escaped for five days from the dreary and hazardous conditions at the Korean front into the dazzle of Tokyo, and were hell-bent on having a number one, fair dinkum, top-line binge, and no messing and to hell with to-morrow; and there were Americans, Canadians, British, Australians, Turks, French and Belgians, Greeks, Indians, Filipinos, Norwegians, and Puerto Ricans, all of the same mind and intentions. Their excited, liquor-loosened babel rose in a crescendo which deafened the brassy caterwauling of the sweating musicians and flowed out of the swinging double doors to mingle with the street noises; the hideous clanking of the tram-wheels over points and the blaring horn-notes of the long columns of sleek American cars which glided like mobile and glittering pachyderms under the winking street-lights of the broad Ginza Avenue.

"This," said Hurst, "is no place for a parson's daughter."

They went out, struggling through the mass, weaving a narrow lane in and out of tables and chairs, squeezing and dodging their way to the entrance, and emerged from the stuffy interior of the beer-hall, gasping into the cool evening air.

"Where to now, Splitpin?" inquired Hurst.

"Don't know, exactly, mate," Edwards said, pushing his cap to one side, a habit he always affected once outside the bounds of retribution; a sort of proxy insult to authority.

"What about that place over the road?" he suggested.

Hurst followed the direction of his pointing finger, and saw on the opposite side of the road an electric sign with the word "Oasis" depicted in fiery-red calligraphy, stationed above an inviting passageway.

"Don't know what's in there," he said, "but it looks right up our street."

Down the passageway was a broad staircase on which little girls were stationed, selling flowers. From below came the strains of music and the murmur of voices; a group of laughing U.S. airmen passed them, on the way up, as they entered a crowded dance-hall.

The military police at the entrance frisked their pockets and scanned their passes. They went in, and sat at a table. All the tables around them were occupied by Servicemen and Japanese girls. Hurst shouted for beer, and sat back in his chair, taking in all the glitter and excitement. The orchestra was larger than the beer-hall ensemble, and more informally dressed in green pantaloons and full, crimson shirts, but essentially they were the same bland, grinning little men, grouped around a polished grand piano in the centre of the stage, playing Western-style music with a faintly Oriental background.

On the far side of the hall under an arch supported by marble pillars a large number of hired Japanese girls dressed in long evening-gowns were chattering gaily to each other, exchanging sly glances under fluttering eyelashes, waiting for dancing partners. As the orchestra struck up with a slow waltz Hurst crossed the floor and parted with a thousand-yen note at a tiny kiosk for a bundle of dance-tickets, and selected a partner.

He chose a girl standing by herself, a little apart, a slender, dark creature with a shape that might have been squeezed out of a tube to specification. Her gown, a creation of filmy white satin which encased her to the knees, and from there swung freely to the ankles, clung rigidly to the outline of her body, and emphasized, rather than concealed, its superbly modulated contours to the point where it plunged into the deep, firm cleft of her breasts. The sandals supporting the arches of her tiny feet were white, and there was a small white rose like a sole star in the night-aspect of the black tresses which reached to the nape of her white neck.

Hurst took her round the floor in a slow waltz to the slow beat of the orchestra, and she danced close to him, so that he could feel the soft impress of her body against his own, gliding across the polished floor, and there was something both of mystery and rapture in the half-open sloe-black eyes which gazed into his.

Breaking into their silent, urgent communion with a slight reluctance, Hurst asked her name, and she replied in a low, vibrant voice that it was Julie, and added, as if it were an additional qualification, "The Americans call me 'the sinner.'"

Fighting down an urge to inquire the reason, Hurst pursued the conversation on other lines, speaking in a subdued voice in tone with the subdued lights of the hall and the muted, drowsy beat of the orchestra.

"What do you do on your nights off?" he asked boldly.

She shook her head very slightly, and the Stygian tresses danced. "No understand. Spik *scoshi* English," throbbed the voice. "I am so sorry."

Splitpin Edwards continued the process of getting drunk which he had commenced earlier in the evening and pursued with steady efficiency, brooking no interference. Having reached the point where his accounting ability began to lose its edge, he no longer occupied his mind in guessing the score to date, and began to look round him for other methods of passing the time. Then it was borne to his befogged mind that the orchestra was in need of a leader—that it was not properly controlled—and once this idea had taken root, it was not long before he had groped his way to the front of the stage and scrambled onto it, and was conducting the orchestra with great verve, with his arms flailing and waving like the limbs of a praying mantis.

For the sake of continuity of narrative it is recorded that later on, much later, when the music had ceased and the grinning musicians were packing up their instruments, and the last of the satisfied patrons of the Oasis were filing through the entrance, Splitpin Edwards, in an ecstasy of conducting his own silent nocturne, fell off the edge of the stage and lay in blissful semi-consciousness on the floor until he was picked up bodily by a couple of military police and bundled into a taxi, whose driver was told to "take Benny Goodman here to the Ebisu Hotel."

*　　　*　　　*

Hurst, by disposing of dance tickets like confetti, made Julie his retainer, and entertained her over soft drinks at a small pine-topped table, and in the passage of an enchanted hour, during which they danced three times without exchanging a word, Hurst was infatuated. She drew him subtly into her world scented by the piquant fragrance of jasmine, a yielding world of soft rustlings and whispered voices, in which nothing grated, yet nothing wholly satisfied, promising more.

Once during a dance he felt the soft brush of her lips against his cheek; and in the long intervals when they engaged in a verbal duel only slightly obstructed by her lack of English, of which she was invariably "so sorry," her dark eyes fascinated and held him.

The hour passed quickly; magically. As Hurst rose to purchase another batch of tickets for the extension of her lease she slipped away, with a promise to return.

When she did return it was in a dramatic fashion, which took Hurst completely by surprise.

It was when the lights were dimmed and only a spotlight played on the area immediately in front of the orchestra that she suddenly appeared from a side-door, dressed in a shimmering golden kimono which became the centre of attraction as soon as she took the floor. Hurst did not recognize her until he had joined the eager crush which formed an arena on three sides to watch her performance, by which time she had shed the first strip of her dress, which was cunningly divided into segments.

The orchestra was stilled, apart from a single clarinet wailing a bolero, to the sensuous music of which Julie danced. She used every inch of her body, from the tips of her tensed fingers down to her quivering ankles, and as the portions of her dress floated away, to fall outside the circle of light which followed her gyrations, the exposed flesh trembled with an ecstasy of emotion.

From the gaping audience there was no sound as the last flimsy wrapping was cast disdainfully away, and she danced on in all the splendour of her young lithe body, naked except for a trio of fig-leaves. Her supple breasts shivered in the delight of their nakedness; her soft lips were parted in a smile of pure joy, exposing a perfection of minute teeth. Her gracefulness was leonine—of the jungle—she was a savage-girl, dancing a fandango in the first light of civilization.

She was exultant; engrossed in herself, and every member of her audience was held engrossed in her, hypnotized by her superb mobile body.

An American sailor broke through the tight cordon and began to sway rhythmically in response to her gestures. He was amazingly agile, and in his close-fitting rig he resembled a lithe puppet moving in a slow circle, just outside the territory of the roving spotlight.

Julie accepted his challenge, and, quickening her pace, danced in a wide arc around him, stretching out her slender arms and tantalizingly withdrawing them when he lunged towards her.

The clarinet took on a new rôle, rising to a faster tempo, hurrying towards a climax. Julie whirled in and out of the sailor's frantic embrace, until finally, in exhaustion, she sank to the floor, one leg extended, her hair falling over her bowed face, in an attitude of abject surrender. Then, as the spotlight faded and the clarinet gave a last despairing note, she was gone like a shadow through the door she had first entered, and the floor, for all its frantic echo of applause, seemed strangely deserted. The sailor, grinning hugely a his own discomfiture, was lost in the throng, and the orchestra blared a quickstep.

Hurst felt lonely and depressed. During the earlier part of the evening he had almost deceived himself into thinking that he shared Julie's confidence with no one, that her eyes, for that evening at any rate, were his alone to gaze at, but during her dance he had glanced around the circle of enchanted faces, and the balloon of that fallacy had burst in his ears. He tore up the remainder of the dance-tickets and made for the exit. As he left he turned to catch a last glimpse of Splitpin Edwards desperately trying to catch up with the frantic extemporization of the saxophones.

XV

"AIKO"

Outside, in the Ginza Avenue, the street was still choked with traffic and the pavements crowded with Servicemen jostled by Japanese touts. One of them was arguing with an aggressive American corporal as Hurst turned the corner from the Oasis; he hesitated, listening. The American was saying, "Ten bucks, you lousy little Nip . . . it never *hatchi*. You'd rob your old granny, you greasy rat! Hey, Chuck!" he appealed to Hurst. "Say, whadya think of this liddle stoat?" The Jap protested shrilly. "I no spik," he whined. "You spik verree nice girl, verree nice 'otel . . ." The corporal gripped him by the shirt and hurled him into the gutter. "Git!" he shouted after him.

He said to Hurst, "Some of these guys'd cut your goddam throat for a nickel. Where you goin', Chuck?"

"Nowhere in partic'lar," Hurst replied.

"What say you an' me team up an' have some fun, bud," the corporal said. He was a youngish man, in his middle twenties, with an athletic frame, tall. "I got nothin' on, either."

"Okay by me," said Hurst. "What name d'you go by?"

"Pete!" said the American. "Put it there, Chuck." They shook hands.

"Just hang on behind, Chuck!" The corporal swung open the door of a cab which waited at the kerb, and Hurst followed him in.

"Hey, you in front, driving this junk-heap," the corporal shouted, "you know a good hotel?"

The driver turned round and said, leering, " 'Otel, boss? Sure, okay."

"Git goin', then, and move, else I'll wring your dirty yellow neck."

The cab moved off and began to swerve at a high speed in and out of the teeming traffic of the Ginza. Leaving the city centre, they entered a maze of narrow streets between low wooden houses crowded together with lighted shop-fronts lining the pavements, and the outlines of moving figures behind the dimly lit plate-glass-enclosed frontages of saké-halls. Here the traffic had thinned out to a trickle, but the passers-by took small notice of the soldiers in the cab. It seemed to Hurst that they went for miles through the tortuous streets of suburbs which were never-ending, but finally they drew up outside a long bungalow with an ornate roof of curved wood tiles. They climbed out into a small square hemmed in by encroaching houses illuminated by the mellow light of street lanterns. A few Japanese loitered in the vicinity of the doorways, the lantern-light giving an unearthly pallor to their inscrutable faces. The American paid off the driver, and they walked across a low veranda to a door which opened spontaneously. An elderly, obese Jap appeared, bowing. "Good e-vening. Pliss come this way." He led them to a small annexe. "Pliss take off your shoes. It is our national custom." They did so, reluctantly. The corporal said, "If they've gone when we come back, so help me . . ." He left the threat unfinished. The Jap smiled tolerantly, bowed again. Two girls materialized, smiling and bowing and giggling. "This way, pliss," the Jap said. Somewhere a gramophone was playing *China Nights*.

After the best night's sleep in months Woodbridge set off from the hotel on the following morning for a shopping tour of Tokyo, and hailed a taxi outside the hotel buildings. The vehicle was battered and dilapidated, powered by a producer-gas generator attached to the rear. In the front seat a woman sat next to the driver, and as Woodbridge opened the door she turned towards him with a gap-toothed smile, and the driver said in a sibilant whisper, "Hey, you and my sister okay, Johnny?"

"No," replied Woodbridge with some heat. "You and my sister not okay, and my name's not Johnny."

"Okay, sucker," grinned the driver. "Where you wan' go?"

"Take me to the PX," Woodbridge commanded.

The American PX building rears its sumptuous façade in the centre of Tokyo's main streets, a six-storeyed emporium dedicated to the luxury of the American occupation forces. The counters lining the great salesrooms are a glittering array of merchandise; of pearls and diamonds, of watches and cameras and silks, of furs, dresses, Japanese arts and crafts, of every conceivable adjunct to modern civilized comfort.

Woodbridge spent two hours in wandering through the building, which swarmed with Servicemen and women, disposing of his small store of American dollar scrip. He had a shoeshine on the first floor, and a haircut on the second; on the third he purchased a dinner service in delicate willow-pattern china, which was crated and dispatched for him on the fourth, while he retired to the basement to dispose of a superbly cooked steak of great proportions in the PX restaurant.

Wandering out into the maze of busy city streets now basking in bright spring sunshine, Woodbridge spent the afternoon gazing into the windows of small shops which were amply stored with Japanese mechanical products and trays of cheap imitation jewellery and porcelain, which had poured from factories staffed by underpaid labour. But here and there, among the less spectacular shop-fronts, he paused as his eyes distinguished from the ruck of indifferent carvings of jade and ivory and wood and the factory-woven embroidered silks, an occasional example of the true art of the Japanese; products of the ancient, half-forgotten age of Buddhist aestheticism, with its subtle blend of simplicity and mysticism.

He made a number of purchases—more than he could afford.

During the evening of the second day in Tokyo Woodbridge attended a recital in the Habiya, the city's largest concert-hall, and found himself placed in a vast gallery which seemed to be occupied largely by Japanese schoolgirls with pigtails, wearing sailor uniforms. The stage, far below, was innocent of curtains, and occupied only by a polished Bechstein grand piano and a tiny stool.

Twenty minutes after the scheduled time for the start of the performance the soloist emerged from the wings, a woman in swirling primose silks, and arranged herself in front of the piano. She began with a Bach cantata, which reached the ears of Woodbridge in a succession of throbbing echoes thrown off at all angles of the great domed auditorium. At each pause the audience gave unrestrained applause, which obscured the first bars of the succeeding phrase.

An American Army major arrived late and sat in a vacant seat next to Woodbridge. He was enthusiastic. "She's good, this kid," he confided. "Wait until she hits Chopin"—he pronounced it 'Show-pan.' "Boy, she's great on Chopin."

When the interval came Woodbridge strolled out on to an outside balcony, lighting a cigarette. Looking down, the whole moving fabric of Tokyo's life was portrayed below, people and traffic swarming among the grey stone buildings of the city area, while farther away among the ugly vistas of the Ginza vicinity the first street lights were flashing like a distant artillery barrage, and Woodbridge shuddered slightly, remembering. In the west, a steely haze of factory smoke took away the glory of the setting sun. Night life was already astir in a city which lived no less by night than by day. . . .

A shrill bell beckoned him back to his seat and to the strident pathos of Chopin, great international

Chopin, interpreted by a Japanese to an American and a Britisher in occupied Tokyo.

In the last work the pianist was partnered by another—a Professor Schreiber, according to Woodbridge's programme—in a rendering of Brahm's Hungarian dances. The professor tottered to the piano, sallow and old, white-suited, and crustily indifferent to the polite applause which greeted his entry. He played an introductory flourish, and waited impatiently for a small girl in a blue dress to place the music on the stand, and seat herself on a stool beside him.

The professor's age belied his agility. His fingers hovered and pounced upon the bass notes, waking tremendous chords which thundered across the hall in waves of billowing sound.

As if stupefied, the small girl turned the page of the score too soon; the professor snatched it back with a rapid turn of his wrist. Terrified, the girl waited too long for the next page, and the professor, in a white rage, ripped it across, and the music continued at a furious pace, the notes mingling into a furious riot of noise, while Woodbridge sat tensed in his seat. Never had he heard music so dominant as this. The aged professor and the slim young woman with her white dumpling of a face all shiny with sweat were playing with all the fire of a full symphony orchestra in a climacteric frenzy.

When the professor struck the final discordant note it was as if the instrument itself broke under the strain of such dire punishment. The entire audience rose and shouted uproar. The small girl ran off-stage and returned with bouquets for the performers.

The professor accepted his without grace, turned it upside down, and gave it back, and tottered into the wings, exuding irritation, mopping his brow with a brilliant green handkerchief.

Nothing lasts for ever, but the five days of Japan leave skimmed by for Hurst and Woodbridge like a small cloud passing across the surface of the sun. They saw little of each other. Occasionally Woodbridge would run into Hurst on his occasional visits to the leave hotel at Ebisu, but their ways did not often cross. Hurst, nearing the end of his leave, hovered between night and day in a perpetual orgy, only aware of the passage of time by the darkness following the light.

Woodbridge spent his time more leisurely, each day acquiring fresh glimpses of the emerging Japanese character, visiting Judo schools, Buddhist temples, and once looking up in awe at the ominous mass of Fujiyama; but when the last day arrived he seemed to have accomplished practically nothing, and the near prospect of returning to the dreariness of the Korean battlefront built up inside him a solid wall of depression.

"Can I help you? What are you looking for?"

Woodbridge glanced up in surprise, for her voice bore no trace of accent. Yet she was Japanese all right, you could tell from the slight set of her eyes, by the dark hair, and she was quite attractive in her neat print dress; but mostly it was the voice.

He was in the library at the Australian Embassy, where he had gone to look at some of the recent editions of his favourite periodicals.

"I was hoping to find a *Mail*."

"But there is one. It is here." She retreated, and returned, bringing it. With faint mockery in her eyes, she asked, "You're not Australian?"

"How did you guess?"

"They ask for the *Mile*."

Woodbridge joined in her laughter.

She retired slipper-footed across the floor to her desk. It was striking three in the street outside. Nobody was in the library except for Woodbridge and the Japanese attendant who spoke immaculate English.

Almost an hour later Woodbridge, as he went out, asked her, "What time do you close down?" not knowing quite what prompted the question, and she looked thoughtfully at him and replied, "Five o'clock to-day, but if you came in before quarter past..."

When he left the building, for the first time he had nowhere to go, and he felt uneasy, impatient. It was his last day. To-morrow...

Woodbridge picked up the 'phone nervously; there were five 'phones in a row, and the other four were being used by Americans, all shouting to drown the station noises. It was five o'clock.

Absurd; he didn't know the number. Idly, because it didn't matter, he flicked over the pages of a directory of occupation-force numbers.

"Yeah, honey," the marine next to him was saying from the corner of his mouth, chewing gum. "Yeah, honey, sure, okay, sugar." A train whistle screamed. Woodbridge dialled the number and listened to the soft burr-burr of the dialling note against the harsh back-cloth of outside interference.

"Jeez, honey," the marine protested. "Course there ain't nobody else . . ."

She picked the receiver up, and her meticulous voice came through. "Hello, sir; this is the library of the Australian Embassy."

"But, sugar . . ."

Woodbridge said in a voice huskier than his own, "Look here, I'm the British soldier who came in this afternoon."

After a pause, "I remember. Is there anything I can do for you?" It was like a doll speaking.

"Yes!" Woodbridge plunged. "You can have dinner with me to-night. I'm going back to Korea in the morning. Will you?"

"Oh!" The voice was startled out of its equanimity; then, in even tones, "I should be altogether delighted."

"Good. I'll pick you up outside in twenty minutes," shouted Woodbridge.

The marine said, "Okay, babe, if that's the way you wan' it." He slammed the instrument on its rest and informed Woodbridge, "Bud, dames is poison."

"Not on your life," Woodbridge said.

A few minutes later Woodbridge, in a taxi, was wondering, Where shall I take her, and what does she eat. Japanese food or European, and what do Japs eat, anyway? He could not remember seeing any Japanese at meals, and was appalled at his ignorance. It was like taking a magpie from the nest, young, only to find that it would exist only on a diet of blackbeetles; what absolute nonsense, anyway, he would soon find out.

*　　*　　*

The subsequent evening passed very congenially for Woodbridge. Aiko—that was her name—proved to be highly versed in European culture, and the conversation as they dined in a quiet corner of a subdued restaurant ranged from Balzac to Lawrence, lingered awhile on politics, dwelt at length upon Elizabethan drama, and touched upon a variety of other, more intimate subjects.

She had developed, she told him in her odd clipped tones, a definite preference for Western foods, with a particular partiality for steak and onions.

It was nearing midnight when Woodbridge eventually piloted her into a taxi, and they drove slowly through the suburbs towards her home.

In parting she said, "I hope you will be able to visit Tokyo again."

Reluctantly, for it was getting late, Woodbridge turned away and watched her from the cab as she turned to smile and wave before disappearing into the gloom between the unlit houses. "Drive on," he said tersely. "Ebisu."

Approaching the centre of the city, he suddenly shouted to the driver to stop. Proceeding at a shambling gait along the street came Hurst, supported on either side by young Japanese girls, who were about to direct his footsteps through the doors of a saké-hall.

Woodbridge tapped him urgently on the shoulder.

"'Allo, corp. I'm aw ri'. Whassa matter?"

"Come on," said Woodbridge. "We leave for the airfield in an hour's time."

"Christ!" Hurst stared at him hard. "What day is it?"

"Friday."

"You sure?"

"Positive."

"Well, s'pose I'd better be movin'." Hurst turned to his escort.

"G'bye, girls, see you some other time."

They looked up at him with sorrowful, cherubic faces. "You go now?" they chorused, incredulously.

"Yes. It's Friday," Hurst explained.

"I am so sorry," one of them said, looking it.

"So am I. Come on, corp." He beckoned Woodbridge to the taxi, and leaned far back in the seat as it picked up speed.

"It was good while it lasted," he reflected. "Bloody good."

XVI

ALL QUIET...

During the first week in April the 29th Brigade left the Yongdungpo area, and moved on through Seoul to positions in the line on the left flank of the U.S. 1st Corps.

Leaving Seoul by the dusty road to the north, the vehicles of the Gloucesters roared past the familiar scenes of devastation, the way littered with the bones of burnt-out lorries and tanks and guns and blasted bridges where detours had been cut through the shallow banks of the dried-up river-beds, on through the town of Uijongbu.

There was a time when Uijongbu was a growing township where light industries flourished, but all these things have passed away.

Never has annihilation been so thorough.

In war cities, towns, and villages are commonly strafed and bombed and battered. Peace comes, and usually from the wreckage of the old sprouts a new community, and in time the scars are healed. But occasionally, as in Uijongbu, there is nothing to build on, nowhere to start, all is rubble, derelict, flat, a wall standing here, a single chimney there, and sometimes a house, but a house without windows, minus half a roof, in imminent peril of falling down. And this was Uijongbu—a place of desecrated human endeavour on a narrow plain between mountains where people once lived and worked, which would not rise again, would never recover its lost status.

As the front line rolled farther to the north the brown squad tents of base units inevitably sprinkled themselves among the ruins, and an area was reclaimed for the building of an airstrip. The U.S. Negro soldiers of the trucking companies and supply groups were the new inhabitants of Uijongbu, and later the parasites of warfare, the lynx-eyed black-marketeers and the slatternly prostitutes, infiltrated in droves from Seoul, and settled temporarily, like a blight, among the few standing ruins of hovels on the outskirts of the town.

But the battalion passed on through the stricken area of Uijongbu, leaving the supply route at Tokchon for a branch route—an appalling hill track which meandered everlastingly in a vague north-westerly direction.

At some places there was scarcely enough width for a single vehicle to pass, and there were times when the drivers had to use all their skill on terribly steep slopes to avoid sliding over the parapets of hundred-foot chasms. The air was full of blinding white dust. Rocks strewed the way. The track advanced ever deeper into the heart of great mountainous ridges which now engulfed it on each side.

The groaning vehicles followed the track for twenty miles, entering finally into a narrow gorge on both sides of which rock-faces rose sheer to hundred-feet heights, and emerged into a valley which followed a stream-bed running like a main artery through a wide range of hills ascending steeply to the region of a thousand feet, where their crests were obscured by wisps of moving grey cloud.

All along the route from the village of Tokchon there had been few signs of human habitation, apart from an occasional small huddle of mud-huts and a few tilled rice-fields wrested from the hill-slopes, and sometimes the isolated dwelling of a charcoal-burner.

Near the spot where the battalion deployed there was one tiny village.

It was called Solma-ri.

Three miles to the north flowed the Imjin river.

Gilmour, who wore the three pips of his recent promotion, stood up in his jeep as the company halted, and wiped the dust from his smarting eyes with a handkerchief.

"God help us if we have to get out of this place in a hurry, Charlie-boy," he said.

For several days the battalion were settling in, digging their defensive positions along the crests of virgin hills, while Colonel Carne strode all day over the area, siting the companies.

Charlie Company dug in on a high ridge overlooking Solma-ri, where Battalion H.Q. were grouped around a stream-bed. Dog Company occupied an extension of the same ridge, where a single large tree dominated the skyline. Baker Company, forward, occupied two features commanding the battalion approaches from the north, and Able, on the left, were situated along the line of a rising ridge running into the blunt promontory of "Castle" Hill, above the village of Choksong.

From Castle Hill the Imjin was visible like an arm sweeping away to the north.

To the rear of the battalion Support Company mounted its positions on a secondary feature, Hill 235, from where the track could be seen winding through the valley for more than a mile, to disappear between a fold in the hills.

Away on the left flank lay the 1st ROK (Korean) Division, and on the right the Northumberland Fusiliers moved up near the river, while the Belgians were established on the other side, where the river made a sudden pocket in the south. The Royal Ulster Rifles were leaguered behind them, in Brigade reserve. The Gloucesters held a frontage of two miles. Between the defending units there were wide, undefended gaps.

But the purpose of the battalions holding these positions in the west was to await the opportunity for attack across the Imjin in the neighborhood of the 38th Parallel, and to press forward into North Korea.

The river itself was thought to be a good defensive barrier against possible assault by the enemy.

And now, in mid-April, there came a burst of spring weather, and the hills were flooded with bright sunshine. Hills which, for all that long winter, had been as barren and bare as volcanic lava on which nothing grows, now began to show a faint aura of green, the bright pastel-green of spring foliage. Later, during the summer, they were to burgeon into a riot of purple and olive semi-tropical splendour, when their shrubbery achieved full foliage; but as yet there were only the first tentative stirrings of young leaves, and the immature opening of wild azalea blossoms on the lower slopes.

In the valleys which wound endlessly between the sheer, tortuous chaos of peaks, apple orchards were beginning to blossom, and the chestnut-trees which were abundant among the valley-slopes were bowed down with heavy, scaly buds.

Animal and bird life began to respond to the sun's comforting warmth.

Flocks of graceful, pure-white herons flew low across the hills towards the river shallows and the flooded paddies beyond to seek for frogs, which, in the areas where they spawned, were already beginning to make the Asian nights hideous with their monotonous quacking chorus.

Magpies, the sparrows of Korea, became noisily attendant to the rearing of their voracious young in the untidy nests among the poplars. Pheasants rocketed away, protesting, from underfoot. High above the two-thousand-feet massif of Kamak-san, the king of its surrounds, a pair of eagles wheeled in their watchful flight, while the lesser kestrels preyed over the fields flanking the river.

Once a deer, to its mortal peril, strayed unconsciously across the battalion front, and peered curiously down from a ledge towards a platoon headquarters where men were brewing tea. It was speeded on its flight by the whine of hunters' bullets.

Towards midday, when the morning mists had cleared, the men, from their points of vantage on the heights, were surrounded by a breathtaking panorama of rolling country stretching as far as forty miles, pierced by the silvery glint of mountain streams caught by the sun, shimmering in a slight heat-haze.

Each day the hills sprang to life as the Korean porters attached to the battalion struggled upward with rations and ammunition strapped to their Everest-packs. Sloan directed the activities of the nine porters who were attached to his platoon.

They were a polyglot collection, wearing all manner of native and Army clothing and equipment.

Each morning Sloan went through a small performance of lining them up for inspection, for the amusement of the platoon.

He would shout, "Attached personnel—'shun!" and their bare legs would come together with a noticeable lack of any sort of cohesion.

"Stand at ease! 'Shun! Wake up, number two! You're the scruffiest individual since Gunga Din croaked!" Number two, not comprehending, would grin with delight at being selected for special abuse.

"From the left—number!" He had taught them their numbers, but their tongues were somewhat unequal to the task of getting round some of the consonants.

"Wan — two — t'ree — soar — size — seex — siven — et —ni-yen. . . ." Occasionally they would purposely give the wrong numbers, "soar—two—et," and collapse with giggling at the torrent of abuse which this manoeuvre brought upon their close-cropped heads.

Then Sloan would go through a pretence of inspection. "Look at your chin, man, it's like a bloody gooseberry. When are you going to shave?"

"Shev?"

"Yes, shave. That beard's five years old if it's a day. Stop grinning, you idiot!"

The first weeks of April passed peacefully in the west. For the first few days Chinese patrols had been observed across the river, but after the arrival of the battalion they had withdrawn. At intervals the 25-pounders sent shells into far distant targets, and several air-strikes went in on positions miles to the north-east, with the Sabre jets just visible, like silvery minnows streaking in and out of tiny puffs of black smoke, but the adjacent hills across the Imjin were silent and brooding heights, showing no signs of any human activity.

Parkington, like most of the troops, grew used to climbing and descending the rugged footpaths to the hilltops.

Mason had now assumed command of the company, with Gilmour as his deputy. On the 18th of the month a fresh batch of reinforcements arrived, which included a subaltern named Tennant, to take over Gilmour's platoon. Mason took him on a tour of the company positions, pointing out the defences.

"Not that it makes much difference now," he said. "I expect we shall be moving across the river in a few days."

"But where are the Chinese reported to be?" asked Tennant, to whom this was a question transcending all others.

Mason pointed north. "Somewhere over there,"

he indicated. "That's all we know. About twelve miles, at a guess, but as to their strength, your guess is as good as mine."

At this period the war in Korea was running down, and becoming static for the first time as the limited offensive of the United Nations gained its objectives, and the opposing armies grouped themselves roughly along the line of the 38th Parallel.

Apart from the outbreak of stubborn fighting in the Chorwon–Pyonggang–Kumhwa triangle on the central front, exchanges began to be confined to patrol encounters all along the front, while the artillery and aircraft of the U.S. Forces continued to seek and destroy; seek and destroy with a consuming hunger which was never satiated.

The dry canker of boredom began to set in among troops who had been too long in the line with too little to do—a factor which had never arisen during the early, desperate days of the long retreat. Unlike the campaigns in which most of the older men had fought, there were no rear areas to which they could retire in reserve, to rest and recuperate and forget for a time the manifestations of battle to which they would soon be returning. It was not like that.

The capital city of Seoul, twice taken, twice relieved, and largely

SMLF Mk. IV

destroyed in the process, showed the first signs of restitution as a fraction of the Korean population seeped back from their refuge in the south, and native shops opened at intervals along the squalid frontages of the streets. Ill-spelt legends in English, such as "Printig and Deevelop" or "Number One Luandry," appeared above their doors to enhance their prospect of hopelessness. More dangerous were the liquor-stalls, which distributed native liquor among passing troops. Some were blinded, some died. A large notice-board, like a gruesome totalizator, was erected in Seoul, keeping the tally of deaths from native hooch, as a warning to the unwary.

On the 20th it was the turn of Parkington's platoon to make an armed reconnaissance across the Imjin; a swan, as it is called in military parlance.

The platoon left before dawn, and were fording the river before the sun had risen high enough to dispel the mists which hung in long rolls above the river-valley. So peaceful was it that Woodbridge pondered vaguely on holiday rambles in the Lake District, for which he had a particular affection.

The line of march was fixed on a feature which became known as Two Graves Hill, and the hill soon rose into their vision, pock-marked by two dominant burial-mounds.

Parkington studied it attentively through his binoculars. There was no movement on it.

"If you see anything moving bigger than a grass-hopper, shoot it," Mason had said. "Then go and find out what it is. Unless, of course, you should run across a battalion. If you do, don't upset them too much. Bring them back here and let us have a go at 'em."

The platoon moved stealthily on, keeping to the lee of the hills which now confronted them, after the low ground of the river-flats. A light wind made whispering noises in the scrub, muffling the noise of their progress. They passed through narrow valleys which might have been well-prepared ambushes, but the sections followed through. Nothing moved on their flanks.

Lane's rifle began to chafe his right shoulder, and he swung it over to the left. Nobody spoke on the march, maintaining the uneasy silence of the hills.

Parkington began to wish for something to grapple with. A tangible objective; the sudden whine of a bullet sending them to ground, or even the friendly whimper of a shell passing overhead towards the distant Chinese positions which nobody could quite pinpoint. But for once the batteries rested.

After four hours the platoon rested and fed on a small hillock to the north of Two Graves Hill, seven miles from the point where they had crossed the river. Parkington searched the neighbouring ground with his binoculars until his eyes ached with the strain, but nothing stirred. At the top of the next rise he noticed signs of recent earthworks, and during the pause, while the platoon rested under the cover of a few stunted trees, he went forward with Sloan to investigate.

*   *   *

They found the reverse slopes of the hill riddled with bunkers connected by a deep trench which zigzagged down to the valley on each side. On the hills opposite the trench began again, stretching like an ugly scar across the broad back of the land-scape.

"Looks at though they're ready to move up any moment," grunted Sloan. "They must have dug this at night." He dropped lightly into the trench and examined the numerous footprints in the soft, sandy soil at the bottom. "Not long been made," he commented.

Parkington wore a frown of bewilderment.

"I wonder what they're up to. . . ." He stared across at the enemy-occupied heights, which now stood out clearly on the horizon. "Perhaps if we stayed here for the night we'd find out."

Thoughtfully, they returned to the platoon, and shortly afterwards started on the journey back. The sun continued to shine throughout the afternoon, and Parkington could not rid himself of the absurd feeling that the surrounding hills were peopled with silent watchers, marking the progress of the patrol. They passed two derelict villages where the rice-fields remained unbroken for the spring sowing, where only a stray Alsatian dog moved among the rubble of the yards. The utter loneliness of the hills communi-cated itself to the spirits of each man.

Half-way to the river they found the letter-box.

Cave, his eyes searching the crests of the hills in front, stumbled over it, almost dropping his rocket-launcher. It was a plain wooden box, sealed, with a rectangular slot in the side. It was the last place they expected to find a letter-box.

Woodbridge shouted, "Careful, it may be a booby-trap." But Cave was already groping inside, and drawing out a sheaf of papers.

They proved to be propaganda pamphlets, written in crude English in long-hand.

Cave read one aloud: "British soldiers, why are you fighting for the greedy profits of the fat capitalists of Wall Street? Lay your rifles down, and join the great democratic movement of free China. This paper will give you protection. It is a free pass to safety. Fight on, and you will be destroyed. . . ."

Cave's serious tones added a ludicrous touch to the forced sincerity of the document, and succeeded in dispersing the gloom which had fallen on the platoon. There was a burst of ironical laughter, and the pamphlets were eagerly sought as souvenirs.

An hour later the tiring sections once more forded the river and filed past the village of Choksong towards their company positions.

XVII

SOLMA-RI

Early on the following day, the 22nd of April, Major Mason left for Kimpo airfield on Tokyo leave, leaving Gilmour in charge of the company. The news of subsequent events at Solma-ri reached his ears soon after he arrived in Japan, and he flew back the next day. By that time there was nothing he could do.

Sergeant Sloan received good news. He was being relieved. A vacancy had arisen in a rest camp which was being set up behind the lines, and his name had gone forward. From now on he would have it cushy, and about time too, he told himself; this was no place for a man over forty with arthritis so bad at times it felt like your bloody veins were on fire. In the comparative sanctity of his dugout he cracked a bottle of whisky, specially stored for an occasion like this, and took a satisfying draught.

All the same, it was a bit of a bind, leaving the lads he had got to know better than their own mothers ever did. And there was young Mr. Parkington: who was going to look after him? Still, —— 'em all, they were old enough to work out their own salvation.

*   *   *

Parkington was at the bottom of the hill, at the jeep-head, watching the colour-sergeant supervising the issue of the evening meal, the men in their heavy-duty cardigans lining up with mess-tins at the ready behind a trio of sweating cooks who were serving the steaming food from hay-boxes, in which it had been preserved during the journey from Forward Echelon, farther along the valley.

The field telephone jangled in its box, and Parkington casually levered out the receiver. "Gilmour here," crackled the voice at the far end. "Company How-Queen. Get all your bodies up on top, Charles, and tell them to stand-to. The N.F.'s are engaging about four hundred Chinks on our left front, and there may be a few heading our way."

"Roger!" Parkington replied.

The day had been a glorious harbinger of summer, and the atmosphere was heavy with a summer warmth even when the sun sank into a cleft of the hills and the shadows lengthened into the brief Oriental twilight. A flock of small birds approaching the battalion positions from the east, like a cloud of polka-dots, veered round in terrified retreat as the 25-pounder spoke with a first sharp crescendo.

The signal operator lay on the ground, earphoned, beside his set, with his cap-comforter pulled well down over his head. He was reading a comic, an old American one, torn and gravel-stained, picked up from God knows where, illuminated by the pilot-light of his wireless-set.

The particular page he was reading concerned

the adventures of Superman, which were so unreal
that his interest was divided between fascination and
scepticism by the vivid imagination of the cartoonist.

Yet somehow his concentration was destroyed by
a strange high pitch of tension, quickening his
pulse-beat. The earphones too buzzed with a fine
sensitivity, and he found that by slightly altering the
wavelength a flow of tangled messages superimposed
themselves upon the anticipatory hum of the con-
densors. The ether was overcrowded—sometimes the
low chant of a Chinese operator broke through faintly,
endlessly... "hubba-hubba-hubba-hubba-hubba-hub-
ba..." in an attempt to jam the signals. Didn't the
bastard ever run short of breath?

Heavy distant explosions, mortar-fire, preceded
by bright orange flashes, persisted over to the right,
seeming to increase in volume. It was near midnight.
There was a full moon; you could see for miles. Something was happening out there, right enough. The
operator shivered with uneasiness. He had heard
that the Chinese always attacked by the light of a full
moon.

"Hobby-horse-one-six for two! One-six for two!
Over!"

The operator became rigidly attentive, and began to fumble in his pocket, eventually producing a
stub of pencil. "Two for one-six. Two for one-six.
Over!" A cigarette, unlit, dropped from the corner of
his mouth. One-six? That would be the ambush
patrol on the river.

"Sunray one-six for sunray two. Have encountered
enemy in estimate battalion strength river-crossing
west two hundred yards. Engaging enemy close range

2″ Mortar

estimate seventy killed no friendly casualties. Ammunition exhausted retiring immediately—out!"

The operator's pencil sped across the surface of the message-pad in desperate anxiety to catch up with the rapid flow of words. Immediately it was set down he scrambled to his feet and walked quickly across the fifteen yards to the Command vehicle. The Adjutant read the message through twice, cocking one eyebrow. He murmured, "Seventy . . . nice going, young Paul."

A few minutes later the artillery were laying down heavy fire on the river-crossing.

Just before midnight the advancing Chinese, fanning out along the valley which flanked the road, encountered Able Company, and the night was suddenly split by a continuous rattle of small-arms fire as their leading sections stormed the forward weapon-pits on Castle Hill, and swarmed among the deserted huts in the village of Choksong.

Parkington's platoon, situated on a spur running parallel to the road, were attacked half an hour later.

Allen, carefully sighting his 2-inch mortar in the darkness, littered the lower slopes with flares, which outlined in sharp relief small groups moving me-chanically towards the crest.

From the cover of his concealed trench Lane raked the hillside with a murderous hail of bullets from his Bren gun at a hundred yards range, sweep-ing backward and forward on a wide arc.

From numerous points in the valley where the Chinese were obscured by darkness, as layers of heavy clouds obscured the moon, a stream of tracer-bullets rose like red-hot sheets of whirling rain, and hissed among the rocks between the dugouts.

"Keep thi' head down," advised Lane to his No. 2, a young National Serviceman named Jenner, who had joined the company three days before on the latest draft. Jenner was rapidly filling magazines as fast as his trembling fingers would allow. Through white lips he asked, "Is it like this very often?"

"Only 'bout once a month. Oi 'ave seen it worse," Lane said casually. "Us'n'll be orl right if 'ee keeps they magazines on the go." A keyholing bullet droned between them and flattened itself against the wall of the trench.

Farther along the ridge, where the company positions were located, Pugh's platoon, in the centre, and Tennant's, holding the right flank, opened fire as the Chinese probed farther along the base of the hills and ascended the gullies which ran towards the upper slopes.

The battle continued through the night. Able Company, who received the first hostile fire, took the greatest weight of the attack. Hundreds of Chinese penetrated their positions and threw themselves suicidally on to their blistering defensive fire. Eventually, by weight of numbers, Able Company were overrun. As the first light flushed the peaks they were ordered to withdraw. Their retreat lay across a patch of open country covered by an enemy machine-gun.

The Company Commander, armed with a pistol and a few grenades, advanced under covering fire and eliminated the gun position. Returning, he was killed by a sniper's bullet.

It was a fine, roseate dawn. The handful of survivors filed out from the Able Company positions above Choksong village and walked wearily into Battalion Headquarters. There were no officers.

It was the 23rd—St. George's Day. St. George for England, and the dragon was the dragon of China. Soon after daybreak the Chinese attacks diminished, apart from occasional short exchanges of fire, and there was a brief lull for the defenders.

But they would return, that was certain. They had withdrawn to regroup—the dragon licking its wounds—but soon the fight would be on again. The entire front was alive. This was the big push all right, with the British 29th Brigade four-square across the middle of the road.

Gilmour took stock. During the night the

stretcher-bearers in Company H.Q., pinned down
by accurate fire, had nevertheless sweated and strained
all night to bring in the wounded in answer to the
urgent calls which had flowed in from the platoons.
Parkington's was worst hit. His casualties were six
killed, twice as many wounded. For Allen, one of the
wounded, it was only a matter of time—a very short
time. A burst of tracer-fire had penetrated his lungs.
A long procession of stretcher cases were borne into
the Regimental Aid Post.

At noon Woodbridge and Hurst were sent back
to Forward Echelon in the Bedford 15-cwt. to evacuate the personal effects of the casualties, and to
return with ammunition. Already stocks were running down.

There was no reserve food. The R.S.M. took a
party of men to scour the vehicles, and returned with
a total of eighteen boxes of combat rations which had
been covered over and forgotten. These were distributed among the six hundred.

Battalion Headquarters moved from the stream-
bed and dug in on a pinnacle overlooking it. A
number of shots and a few mortar-bombs had fallen
among their bivouacs during the day, and they had
become untenable. The Chinese might, under cover
of darkness, infiltrate along the valley.

At Forward Echelon, seven miles along the valley, Woodbridge and Hurst loaded their vehicle with
ammunition at top speed.

Mr Prestcott, the SO2, had told them, just
before departing himself in the Signals three-tonner
with fresh batteries, "Don't hang around longer than

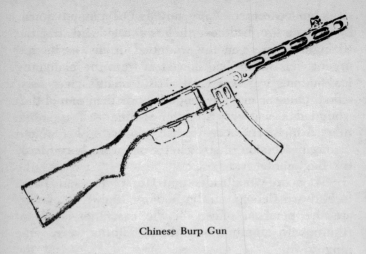

Chinese Burp Gun

you can help. We expect to lose physical contact with the battalion soon." He meant physical contact as distinct from wireless contact. He meant that the Chinese had probably cut the road, and in this he was right.

At three o'clock Hurst started the Bedford and nursed it over the rough ground of the battalion supply route. They had gone nearly a mile when a swaying ambulance approached them over the twisting track, slackening speed in order to squeeze past. The driver, white-faced, shouted something unintelligible, but the meaning was not lost. It was manifest in the patternless rows of neat holes which were scattered across the body of the vehicle. Hurst pulled up. "Want to go on?" he asked.

Woodbridge said, "He got through, didn't he?"

Hurst replied, "'Ope there ain't too many of 'em, that's all."

He let in the clutch; the Bedford rolled forward.

Three miles on, as they rounded a bend of the track, the Signals three-tonner was visible, overturned in a gully by the roadside, with flames licking the cab. A small group of white-clad figures were clustered under a rock-face at fifty yards distance, and as they came on bullets droned about their heads like disturbed hornets. Woodbridge loosed a wild round in their direction, the explosion vibrating enormously in the confined space of the cab. Hurst urged the Bedford over the rugged surface of the track at a speed which strained every rivet to its breaking-point. Still running the gauntlet of fire, they passed the hostile group under the hill, and then they were round the next bend. Bullets had shattered the windscreen, ploughed through the instrument panel, splintered the steering-wheel.

Another harsh chattering of fire from close at hand; the engine cut out as if it had been abruptly switched off, and a thin column of steam rose from the engine-cowling. Hurst steered off the road into the cover of a slight dip. Woodbridge climbed out hurriedly, rifle cocked, and wriggled into the surrounding scrub. Over the lip of a shallow ditch he glimpsed the head and shoulders of a Chinese in a trench by the roadside, and the blunt muzzle of a Burp gun, searching the ground to his left. Slowly Woodbridge raised his rifle and took careful aim. The enemy soldier saw the movement just as he pressed the trigger, and threw himself sideways, aiming a burst at Woodbridge as he did so. A round from the Burp gun knocked the rifle spinning into the open, and sliced a small splinter of bone from his thumb.

Hurst called in a low voice, "Are you all right?"

"Yes, I'm okay, but the rifle's gone, and he's got us covered. Where's your Sten?"

"Under the bus. What's the next move?"

"We can't get away. There's no cover. Have to give ourselves up."

"Rice for breakfast," Hurst said dismally.

Early that day the battalion had been drawn in to a tighter perimeter. Gilmour's company, under constant attack themselves, gave covering fire as Baker withdrew into Charlie Company's positions, and then, bitterly, he watched his platoon filing down the hill which they had held stubbornly through the night on to a less exposed feature near Hill 235, to the south of the road. In the stream-bed below, C Troop of the 170th Mortar Battery remained, waiting for instructions to move to new positions. Since the onset of the offensive they had shattered the peace of the area with a hail of bombs without a respite. Their instructions, if they came at all, came too late.

The Belgians, across the river on the Brigade right flank, battled through the 23rd against masses of Chinese passing across their front, and infiltrating between their rear and the river. Farther west thousands streamed across to attack the forward companies of the R.N.F.'s, advancing through the undefended valleys on their left flank towards the towering mass of Kamak-san in the distance, while the 25-pounders of the 45th Field Regiment and the remaining troops of 170 Mortar Battery grouped around Brigade Headquarters barked their volleys of destruction without pause.

X Company of the Fusiliers withdrew from their isolated position. Shortly afterwards Z Company were partly dislodged from their entrenched positions by a strong frontal attack, and their subsequent counter-attack was repulsed by weight of numbers.

The position was now becoming rather grave, with the Belgians all but surrounded in front, and Y Company on a precarious limb over to the left; and when the heavy Patton tanks of the 65th R.C.T. failed to throw the Chinese from their foothold on Z Company position the Northumberlands fell back into a closer formation around their Battalion Head-quarters, protecting the supply route—the line of retreat—and Y Company withdrew safely from their forward position to strengthen the battalion line.

The tanks advanced to the Imjin in support of the Belgians, who retired across the river on the right, after resisting all attempts of the Chinese to pierce their defensive system, and took up new positions in the rear. The Royal Ulster Rifles advanced to contact from their reserve positions, and occupied the hills on the other side of the supply route. A troop of Centurions of the 8th Hussars rumbled into the Brigade front, prepared for instant action. The Chinese, who now overran the adjacent hills in numerous small groups, converged upon the defended area of the three battalions, and returned to the attack.

With daylight gradually waning the Gloucesters were holding their shortened line against persistent attacks from three sides.

Their supply route was cut. Late in the afternoon Forward Echelon, the advanced base for supplies and transport, had been attacked by the first elements of enemy troops coming down through the central gap in the Brigade front. They were dressed in white peasants' smocks, but their activity left little doubt of their real intentions. The skeleton staff of the echelon contrived to hold off the attack until the drivers had kicked their vehicles into life, and in the midst of a sporadic hail of bullets they leaped aboard and departed in a heavy cloud of dust towards the security of A Echelon, several miles to the east, with most of their vehicles intact.

XVIII

CUT OFF

Throughout the night of the 23rd the Chinese, heavily reinforced, pressed their assault on the Gloucester position.

On the ridges held by Baker and Charlie Companies fierce grenade and small-arms battles were fought. In the flickering light of flares and the sudden glaring flash of explosives, the defenders glimpsed masses of the enemy swarming at the bottom of the hill.

It was a long night; one of the longest in the history of war.

When the pregnant darkness was relieved by the light of dawn on the 24th it came as a merciful relief to the tired survivors—the removal of the hot poultice of constant alarm; of eyes straining through the darkness; of firing alike at shadows which shrieked and close, solid forms which toppled silently; expecting at any moment the penetrating impact of a bullet, equivalent to a heavy punch in the guts. . . .

The Chinese fell back, repulsed, leaving fresh heaps of their dead encumbering the lower slopes of the hills, while the battalion stretcher-bearers evacuated the groaning wounded from their slit-trenches.

A helicopter, called in to take out the seriously wounded, hovered over the scene, and finally, finding no safe spot for descent inside that small ring of flying steel splinters, faded slowly out of sight to the south.

The fifteen men of Baker Company who had survived the night limped painfully out of their foxholes and retired to dig new positions on Hill 235.

The night had been bitterly cold, with a hard frost, and Hurst and Woodbridge spent it rolled up in a single blanket on a high crag near the supply route where they had been taken prisoner, guarded by their captors. Mr Prestcott and three other men who had been taken in the vicinity of Forward Echelon slept near them, in the same small hollow. In the morning they rose at first light, shivering, stamping their feet. The Chinese guards looked on goodhumouredly, as if they appreciated and knew themselves, only too well, what it was like to be cold.

Since their capture they had been treated with an odd deference. True there was always, in the background, a small padded Chinese with a Burp gun in the crook of his arm; they had been stripped of all their valuables; but the platoon-sized force with whom they were now quartered appeared to be tolerant, even amused at their discomfiture. One, grinning, had patted Hurst's shoulder in a friendly, patronizing manner and addressed words to him which seemed to convey sympathy. Hurst had turned round with his teeth bared in a forced grin and replied in a tone of mock resignation, "Get ——ed, you slant-eyed little bastard," and the Chinese had bowed politely.

They were taken to an officer, who addressed them in stilted, platitudinous English. "You are prisoners of the Chinese Communist Forces. ("Tell us something we don't ——ing-well know," Hurst growled.) Do not try, pliss, to escape, or you will be shot like a dog. You will be well fed if you do not try to escape."

"Well fed?" echoed Hurst, whose prophecy of rice for breakfast had not so far come true.

Prestcott, when the Chinese officer was out of earshot, said casually, "Keep on your toes; there may be a chance to get away. If you manage it on your own, make for the battalion, or Brigade H.Q., if you can't reach it."

Later in the morning Prestcott was taken to a near-by pinnacle for interrogation.

It was going to be another fine day, Woodbridge thought, gazing up at the portents in the sky, and listening to the echo of gunfire farther along the valley.

His eyes caught the glint of a small circling aircraft, high overhead, wheeling like a watchful hawk.

The three Mustangs of the U.S. Air Force swept over at a considerable height and peeled off individually to come in to the attack. Woodbridge had time to shout, "Get under cover!" as the twin canisters of napalm dropped from the wings of the leading aircraft a hundred yards farther down the slope. They burst with an angry, swelling roar, sending a rippling well of jellied fire streaming out from the centre.

A white-hot wave of lava surged downhill, dribbling among the gullies, and over the lips of the slit trenches, dancing in little tongues of flame on the rocks, searing and sizzling in the thick, dry scrub.

The Chinese were taken by surprise and plunged into utter confusion. They scattered and went to ground in all directions. One, licked by flames from head to foot, ran screaming past the group of captives into the thick of the conflagration now raging in a small grove of blackened sweet-chestnut trees. The air was full of the soft, insinuating sound of frizzling, as if boiling fat had been poured over the ground.

A flying figure burst into the open and made a headlong dash for the valley. It was Prestcott. The second Mustang zoomed low, flattened out, dropped its canisters. A rising pillar of fire blotted out the sight of Prestcott as he turned off in the direction of the battalion lines.

Woodbridge shouted, "Let's go!"

The six men scrambled up and sprinted to the bottom of the hill. A single shot whined between them. Running hard, they rounded the contour of the hill, crossed the valley, and took refuge in a cluster of trees on the far side.

"Listen!" Woodbridge said, as they recovered their wind. "We're not out of the wood yet. All the hills leading to the battalion are occupied, so we'd best make our way east and try to get to Brigade Headquarters. We'll go in single file, and pretend we're still in captivity until we get out. It's about our only chance. Agreed?" Only one man dissented, a driver, Briggs. He was overruled.

Woodbridge leading, they set out in file, using all the available cover, through the valleys leading to

the east. As they passed through a narrow defile
there was movement on the hills above, and it became obvious that the slopes flanking the defile were
populated.

"Too late to go back," Woodbridge said. "Keep
moving."

They walked on slowly, keeping in file.

A platoon of Chinese watched them with great
curiosity. Woodbridge's damaged hand was held in a
crude sling improvised from a piece of white flannel
given to him by his captor. Another man had a
bandaged head. Hurst affected a limp.

As they slowly passed between the occupied
slopes a Chinese shouted something unintelligible.
Woodbridge, with a defeated grimace, pointed downward with his good thumb. In reply he shouted the
first word which came to his mind.

"Officer!"

The Chinese nodded, grinning.

Briggs said in a hoarse undertone, "For Christ's
sake let's run for it. They'll shoot us down like rats."

Hurst, who was nodding and smiling back at the
Chinese, said savagely from the corner of his mouth,
"Shut up, you stupid bastard!"

The enemy troops, leaning on their arms, rocked
with high-pitched laughter as the pitiful file of ragged
men approached a bend in the valley and passed
slowly out of their vision round the edge of a small rise.

Three hours later, after patient reconnaissance,
sudden dashes across open spaces, trembling intervals crouched under cover, and weary detours over
mountain-paths, the six men stumbled into Brigade
Headquarters.

*   *   *

For the remnants of Parkington's platoon the night had been relatively quiet, although there had been no opportunity to relax—to snatch a precious hour's sleep. Shortly after morning Gilmour slipped quietly into Parkington's slit-trench.

"It looks pretty bad," Parkington commented.

"You can underline that." Gilmour lit a cigarette. "Might as well have it now. It's my last." He had given the rest away on the previous day. "We're up the creek, Charlie-boy, up the creek and without a bloody paddle, unless they get a relieving column through."

"Any more news?" Parkington asked.

"Not much we don't already know. We're surrounded, of course, and the rest of the Brigade has had it pretty rough. I believe they're trying to organize something for this afternoon. And there's an air-drop laid on for supplies. Apart from that, anything can happen."

Parkington forced a grim smile, and when Gilmour had gone to visit Pugh's platoon, on the next spur, his mind, for the first time, dwelt upon the situation they were now in. . . .

Well, they had bought it, as the saying went. It was a pity, in a way—in a very localized and personal way—that the Chinese had chosen to hinge their spring offensive on this point, but in the long run it was a good thing. Good, because they would lose a division, and nobody could afford a division on the subjugation of a battalion, not even the Chinese, with their enormous reserves of gun-fodder. And the other battalions—they would have time enough to wriggle out of the net, they would fall back and face the depleted Reds on another line, miles to the rear, halt them, and throw them back again, and the next time they would put a division here, where a brigade had once been overrun.

The battalion itself was doomed, which was a pity, because it was a good battalion, but, all the same, you had to get the thing into focus on a wider scale, in proper perspective. It was only your own little bit of the apple which had gone bad, and had to be cut off to avoid infecting the rest. Meanwhile, as Gilmour had said, a lot of good men would go west, filled full of little holes for the sake of freedom, ten thousand miles from everything the word signified. *Decorum est pro patria mori*. Of course, it was right that some had to die. . . .

A discordant chorus of bugles sounded away to the right. They were coming again. "Stand by!" he shouted. "Let 'em have it."

Sloan distributed the last boxes of ammunition to the sections, and sat wearily on an empty box in his dugout. During the previous night he had expected to hear the order to pack up and prepare to break out, before it was too late, but now the time for that was past. He had known it was too late early in the day, when he had looked out across the hills to the south as the mist was rising from the valleys and the distant slopes were exposed, chequered with patches of vegetation. In the foreground, about a mile away, stretched a neck of land, a low, flat saddle between two hills.

On closer scrutiny the light background of this

plateau was broken by masses of moving figures, black against the sun, moving forward in long line abreast, wave after wave, like a swarm of locusts moving over the surface of a desert. The sight had raised a wild hope, quickly dashed when Sloan brought his binoculars to bear, and identified a regiment of Chinese infantry. There was to be no retreat. The certainty came as a relief to his taut nerves; previously there had been an unbearable tension about the atmosphere, steadily increasing, like the moment of suspense between a flash of lightning and the answering peal of thunder, but now, to Sloan, there was the certainty of fighting on to the end.

Lane took two small ration-tins from his pouches.

"Beef stew or pork and gravy?" he asked. "'Tis the lot."

Jenner said, "Let's eat it later. There might not be any more."

"There won't, that's a fact. Wha's the use of waitin'? You might be bloody-well dead in 'alf an hour."

Reluctantly Jenner took the proffered tin.

Three of the battalion's Vickers machine-guns remained in action, having fired almost continuously for two days. Once a company of Chinese emerged round a bend in the track, mounted on bicycles, pedalling furiously into the centre of the Vickers' field of fire, and two of the guns had opened up simultaneously with a sustained burst.

The cranking-handles flew backward and forward as the belts snaked through the feed-blocks and the steam from the water-jackets poured through the condensor-tubes into the water-cans as the barrels rapidly became very hot.

The result was almost comical.

The company of cyclists piled up on the road-sides in a writhing chaos of flailing limbs entwined with wheels and handle-bars under the devastating crossfire of the Vickers. At that crucial moment the 25-pounders picked up the bearing, and a hail of shells straddled the road.

One of the Vickers, virtually exposed on a high pinnacle of rock, pumped belt after belt into the enemy positions until spent cartridge-cases, falling off like dead leaves, formed a thick carpet covering the surrounding area. The Chinese directed a storm of fire on the gun position, but miraculously the gunners survived, holding up all attacks on their flank and killing hundreds of the enemy troops who thronged the opposite slopes, until, eventually, in the closing stages of the battle, the barrel seized in its bearings through lack of water.

Early in the afternoon a squadron of Filipino tanks, supported by infantry, advanced slowly along the supply route to the battalion between the precip-itous hills, which grew more formidable as they progressed. Fighting off light opposition from small forces of Chinese encountered along the route, the relieving column groped its way along the appalling road, steadily nearer to the positions where the Gloucesters were beleaguered. Two miles from their objective, on the crest of a steep dip where the track narrowed to a mere ribbon, and became a ledge hacked from a mountain-side, bounded on one side by a precipice, the leading tank struck a mine and was disabled, blocking all further passage.

With great reluctance the tanks were put into reverse, and the column swung round and retired to the east. The faint and unmistakable rumble of tank engines was carried on a light breeze to the ears of the men trapped on the heights above Solma-ri.

Later columns of Centurion tanks, with U.S., Puerto Rican, and Belgian forces, endeavoured to force a way through to the battalion, but in the end the mountainous country proved insuperable.

The air-drop too was a failure. A few light aircraft flew over the position, and dropped medical supplies, ammunition, and Bren guns. The ammunition-boxes rolled down the hillsides out of reach of the defenders, and without ammunition the Brens were useless. Later a trio of U.S. flying boxcars, resembling huge and ponderous flying beetles, flew across the area with a larger cargo, but they could not penetrate the umbrella of fire which encompassed the surrounded battalion, whose effective fighting

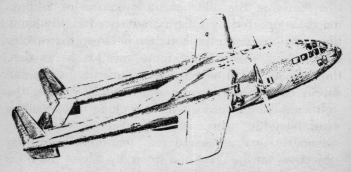

Fairchild C 119 "Flying Boxcar"

strength had now shrunk to no more than three hundred men.

Throughout the 24th the Chinese mounted their attacks, which were persistently held off by a murderous screen of fire from the defenders, by the pinpoint accuracy of the 25-pounders, and the continuous air-strikes of the U.S. Air Force, operating a day-long shuttle-service of destruction, razing the enemy-held slopes and valleys with high explosives, napalm, rockets, and cannon-shells. Once Sloan, leading one of his sections in defence against a fresh assault, saw a Sabre jet swoop in to drop a napalm bomb fifty yards from his front line of defence. The napalm exploded in a blast of searing flame, and one of the attacking Chinese was catapulted fifty feet upward from its centre of impact.

Sloan observed that as he reached the zenith of his flight the enemy soldier burst suddenly into flame, and fell to earth like a blazing faggot.

The 4.2-mortar troop, who had abandoned their positions by the stream-bed, withdrew across the track and dug new defences on Hill 235, dismantling the heavy barrels of their mortars, and dragging them up the rugged slope. Soon after their withdrawal the 25-pounders laid down a salvo of shells on the vehicles which were left in the valley after the supply route had been cut, destroying them utterly.

The Chinese were unlikely to capture any worthwhile booty.

XIX

"WE ARE OPERATIONAL"

As dusk fell, and the bombardment slackened a little, Colonel Carne ordered the withdrawal of the battalion survivors to Hill 235—Gloucester Hill—for the final stages of the battle.

In small groups they passed through Parkington's platoon, toiling slowly towards the summit, stumbling over the twisting hill path, eyes red with loss of sleep, and under-scored with dark patches of sleeplessness, the smoke-blackened skin of their faces drawn tight with strain, their movements jerky, walking with mechanical effort.

The men of Parkington's platoon, through the deep fog of their own tiredness and exhaustion, threw occasional witticisms at some of the men they knew, but most were content to exchange weary grins of acknowledgment.

Soon after darkness had fallen, the battalion was firmly entrenched on Hill 235, with the wounded laid out in a slight hollow near the crest of the hill.

The supplies of food and water had long since been consumed. The batteries of the two remaining wireless sets which formed the sole link with Brigade headquarters were running down.

There was very little ammunition.

"After this lot," Cave said, "I'm finished." He said it casually, with a shrug of his shoulders, with exaggerated finality.

Crouching next to him, in the gloom, Powell observed, "Don't know what you're m-moaning about, you ain't m-married. I've got three ker-kids." To Cave, his companion's stutter seemed incongruous in this half-light of stark reality. He changed the topic. "'Eard a rumour from one of the blokes in Charlie Company. Says the Chinks 'ave trained a band of apes to throw grenades. One of 'is mates shot one yesterday, sort of gorilla, hairy all over."

Powell stared. "You f-feeling all right, Cavey?" he inquired anxiously.

During the evening the Chinese launched a heavy assault on the hill, sending in successive waves of infantry, while a rain of mortar-bombs fell on the harassed defenders. Still the line held. Jenner, the recruit, was killed by a grenade which burst in the trench where Lane continued to keep up a withering fire from his Bren gun. Cave died in the open, riddled by carbine bullets directly after his eyes, piercing the darkness, picked out a section of Chinese advancing in a small arc. Powell, who saw him fall, wiped out the section with grenades, in a savage frenzy of activity. The Chinese attacked incessantly through the night. At dawn Parkington mustered fifteen of his platoon still in action—less than half of its original strength. Pugh and Tennant were rather better off. Gilmour's company, with eighty sound men, were by far the strongest in the battalion.

As the sun rose and the contours of the eastern hills were etched in dark shadow, softened by patches of drifting mist, the artillery barrage which closed round the vital hill throughout the night suddenly lifted for a short time, and a strange stillness fell, punctuated only by the occasional whine of a stray bullet.

The drum-major was ordered to blow his bugle.

The unwavering notes rang out in solemn silence. He blew reveille, and followed with a concoction of other calls—post, jankers, fire—and, ironically, cookhouse. From all sides of the barren hill slopes the survivors rose up and cheered, waved their arms, shouted defiance in a great infectious surge of feeling.

As the last note died it was succeeded by the harsh crackle of small-arms fire, and the men of the Gloucesters, refreshed in spirit, settled again behind their rifles and machine-guns to ward off another fierce attack on the Able Company sector.

Soon after daylight the air strikes began anew, and the enemy troops who invested Hill 235 momentarily withdrew into cover to regroup.

By this time the South Korean Division on the left of the 29th Brigade had been pushed back for several miles, and the hills far to the south of the Gloucester position had been overrun by hostile forces. It was obvious that the battalion, or what remained of its fighting strength, would soon be out of ammunition, after three days of continuous fighting, even if its indomitable spirit could sustain it indefinitely.

On the hill the men were carefree in the casual manner of men who had nothing to lose, were beyond fear, and, having lived with violence and death for so long a time, now had come to regard it with equanimity.

At six o'clock, on the fast-fading radio, permission to break out was received from the Brigade Commander.

Their epic stand, having achieved its end, was over. Only the Gloucesters could have done it....

The Chinese had relentlessly increased their pressure all along the Brigade front, and during the 24th the Ulsters, the Northumberlands, and the Belgians fought to maintain their position against the repeated attacks of the strong Chinese formations which came across the northern hills, and swarmed through the west in the region of the massive feature of Kamak-san in an effort to cut off the battalions, and sever the main supply artery which ran southward to Uijongbu.

By the time orders to withdraw were received the Brigade were virtually surrounded, and there began a tense struggle to disengage in the face of constant attack. The Northumberlands retreated through the supply route held by the Ulsters, supported by a troop of Royal Engineers whom force of circumstances had turned into infantrymen.

As they entered a narrow pass the Chinese stormed the overhanging heights, and surged round the borders of the road. Eventually they were thrown back, but the Northumberlands lost their Commanding Officer, and the pressure was now so great that the road could not be held until all units had passed safely through. A squadron of Centurions, squat and massive, moved cautiously along the valley in support of the withdrawal.

The Ulsters and a few remaining details of Northumberland Fusiliers were struggling to maintain their hold on the heights commanding the route, and they now fell back as the 20-pounder guns of the Centurions pounded the opposing forces.

The heavy tanks had little room to manoeuvre on the narrow track flanked by paddy-fields and steep ditches, and the Chinese were running down from the slopes under a hail of bullets from the machine-guns under the turrets. Mortar-bombs began to throw up fountains of earth along the track. Several of the tanks floundered in the soft mud of the paddies.

The Chinese had cut the line of retreat near the pass, the only route available for the Centurions. As the tanks approached, escorting the retreating infantry, a desperate fight ensued.

The majority of the riflemen turned off across the eastern hills and made their way out over open country. Others, including the wounded who could not walk, mounted the tanks and ran the gauntlet of fire which the Chinese, swarming in ambush, poured into them. Several of the tanks were disabled. Most of the passengers were killed. Blood ran in rivulets over the turrets and dripped into the dust of the

25-Pounder

road. One of the Centurions wheeled on a Chinese lying in the road behind a machine-gun and crushed him into the earth as a beetle is crushed underfoot, without dignity. Another crew, observing through their periscope that a Chinese was clinging to the turret, burst through a flimsy wooden shack by the roadside, which effectively removed the unwanted guest.

The Belgians, who were also contesting for their right to disengage, retired in close contact to the east.

The enemy, whose numerical strength was now overwhelming, followed up the withdrawal for several miles, and the Centurions engaged them in a running battle as the haggard men of the 29th Brigade converged upon the road to Uijongbu.

*   *   *

During this period the A Echelon of the Gloucesters, situated on the bend of a small river near
Tokchon, raised a carrier force of every available
man—cooks, drivers, storemen—to support the withdrawal of the 25-pounder gun crews of the 45th
Field Regiment, who were coming under fire in their
position not far from Brigade Headquarters.

The carriers rumbled away quickly, and in half
an hour had reached the spot where the gunners
slaved at their smoking guns in support of the battalions which still held out at Solma-ri. Bren guns were
fixed to the gun-mountings, trained on the threatening hills beyond where the Chinese were fanning out
and moving south and east. The Echelon men took
up positions on the surrounding slopes just as the
gunners received the order to withdraw.

In a few minutes the guns were dismounted,
and hitched, with their ammunition trailers, to the
vehicles. They moved off with a rousing cheer for the
infantrymen, at top speed, not wasting a moment.

Time, on that day, was at a high premium.

While the first shots of the oncoming enemy
hummed over them the supporting troops also withdrew, following the gunners out towards the supply
route.

When they reached the village of Tokchon the
gunners deployed once more in a paddy-field, mounted their guns, and unloaded the remaining ammunition. Brisk orders were shouted. Sights were set. At
a given word the barrels again spurted flame with an
angry crescendo, hurling a heavy salvo of shells far to

the west—towards the surrounded men of the Gloucesters.

For fifteen minutes the intensive barrage continued, each team firing shell after shell with superb precision.

Only when the last round was expended did the gunners wearily dismount their pieces and pull out along the route to Uijongbu, in the south, a long, triumphant column of silent men and guns.

From Chorwon, in the north, down through Tokchon and Uijongbu, and hence to Seoul, runs a valley, narrow at first, but widening to the dimensions of a plain as it continues on its devious course.

The plain is the more prominent because it is very flat, and interlarded with a network of streams and dikes watering the paddy-fields which abound in the fertile soil of this low ribbon of land, and because the hills which march alongside are particularly gaunt and bare, only partially clothed with vegetation, showing large bald patches of smooth black rock and red sandstone.

Through this valley have swarmed the hordes of the history-book conquerors of Korea; it was the route selected by Genghis Khan in the dim past.

Through this natural gap the Chinese, unchecked, would have poured to seize the vital road junction at Uijongbu, cut off and outflanked the whole of the 1st Corps, and swept on to celebrate the Red festival of May Day in the sparsely defended capital of South Korea.

In the afternoon of the 25th of April the plain

above Tokchon was streaming with retreating troops who had helped to spoil the Chinese offensive at its outset. The Brigade, out of contact, was falling back towards Tokchon, and they walked alongside the road, limped across the terraced paddy-fields, and stumbled over the low foothills, some without arms, grimy and grim, men who had not shaved for days and badly needed sleep, several with wounds needing urgent attention.

Yet the danger was not yet past, and at the crossroads in Tokchon they formed up again, regrouped, and took up defensive positions in the low hills near the village.

At last, just before midnight, the Brigade was relieved by an American regiment, and the men, drooping with fatigue, were taken out of the line and conveyed by lorries back to Seoul.

At approximately nine o'clock on the morning of the 25th, during a comparative lull in the fighting, Colonel Carne held a final O-group with the remaining Company Commanders, in a small hollow. It was decided that each company should attempt a break-out, and the Colonel suggested a route to the south. Gilmour elected to strike north, and turn south-west, and the remainder of the battalion formed a single unit and prepared to evacuate from the hill. The Colonel, the Chaplain, the Medical Officer, and the R.S.M. stayed with the wounded to await the coming of the Chinese.

Gilmour assembled his company, and as they formed up they stood watching the departure of the other companies. They comprised a force of less than two hundred men. They moved off slowly, mounting

Sten Gun

the crest of the hill and disappearing in small groups below the skyline, making for the high ground to the south, which was now densely populated by enemy troops.

Gilmour consulted his watch. It was still going, although he could not remember when he had last wound it. To the small group of men who were about to leave he said, "We're going to try to break out. It will probably be tough going, If some of us get shot up, the remainder will have to carry on, and nobody will be picked up. The wounded will have to stay."

There was a murmur of assent.

Each carrying a rifle or Sten gun, the company filed off through the scrub and followed Gilmour across the valley at the foot of the hill, striking deeper into enemy territory.

Lane, who walked to the rear of the column, was moving mechanically; there was no feeling in his body. All the ache of his tiredness seemed to have melted away, worn itself out, and his legs were numb in their locomotion, as if he walked upon stilts. He had been rendered completely deaf by the continuous noise of his Bren gun, so that there was a corresponding numbness in his head, and a faint, high-pitched hum, like the singing of a tuning-fork.

From this dead chrysalis of his physical faculties emerged his thoughts with the clearness and brightness of butterflies' wings.

Impressions persisted in invading a certain strange country of his mind which was a long way from reality, mingled with a painful longing to be somewhere else, away from the carnage he had seen wrought.

Why, couldn't he just see himself on that last stretch of line on the way home, after the last of the big stations, all noise and bustle, and the little daisy-covered pocket-handkerchiefs of meadows, and the big placards telling you that you were going into the Strong country? And the small stations which the train would flash past, hardly ever stopping unless it was slow from Bath—Oldfield Park, Saltford, Keynsham, Somerdale.... His lips formed the names soundlessly. There was a prospect before his eyes of a small common on fire with the yellow flames of gorse, narrow strips of gardens flanking the track, and the grey country houses set back a little way....

Sloan's mind dwelt wholly, alertly, on self-preservation. His eyes feverishly searched the hills and valleys. Overhead, flying high, a Harvard droned. It was alone in a clear sky.

Underneath dead men were scattered all over the hill-slopes, but the Harvard was aloof, secure from all that.

Sloan was vaguely irritated that the aircraft, so near, was yet not included, as they were, in a steel-jawed trap. Uppermost in his mind was the determination to break out. The order was to escape. Had it been to fight on until you were killed, or dropped from exhaustion, Sloan would have done so without question. His mind was conditioned over long years of service to obedience and to command; authority was his god; there was no room for emotion.

For two miles, oddly, they met few enemy. One, emerging from behind a rock to confront the entire company, challenged them defiantly, with his carbine canted towards them.

"Shoot that bloody man!" bellowed Gilmour.

A ragged volley of rifle-fire; the Chinese crumpled into the earth, his expression frozen into a rigid mask of defiance.

Soon afterwards two more Chinese were shot as they scrambled out of a slit trench, and another, making off to raise the alarm, was shot down in flight.

Once when a whole platoon of Chinese were encountered on a near hill the company took cover, but the enemy platoon hastily scrambled out of sight, in fear, and left them to continue their journey in peace.

After an hour Gilmour came to a rock-strewn stream, and he followed the course of it, veering south. Finally, after four miles of rough going, they entered a long, straight valley.

During their passage there had been an uncanny peace; this was broken, as every man knew it would be broken before the end.

Spontaneously machine-guns stuttered from the

hills on each side of the valley. A number of men fell. The remainder took cover in a shallow ditch full of stones and coarse shrub.

Above them in the hills a battle was raging between the Chinese and the South Koreans, who were beginning to crumble into rout.

Lane was among the first of the casualties. As he made for the ditch he was hit several times in the thighs. He rolled over into the low bushes and lay still, watching the progress of his fellows. When he moved his legs sharp stabs of agony ran the length of his spine. So he did not move, but lay still, feeling a slow paralysis creeping through his body, and a great drowsiness. He could see the Chinese soldiers running down from the hill to attack the rear of the column, but he was not worried by this. His mind was a great distance away.

The Harvard dipped its wings and swept across the brow of the hill, dropping small canisters on the slopes which belched smoke. A flight of Sabre jets suddenly materialized and streaked below the level of the hills, raking the enemy with cannon-fire. At the far end of the valley a squadron of American tanks were approaching.

Half-way along the valley the ditch petered out, and the survivors ran towards the tanks across open territory. The Chinese fire was intense, and the bewildered Koreans also fired into the valley.

The tanks advanced along the valley, pouring machine-gun fire into the straggling band of men coming towards them. Several of them fell.

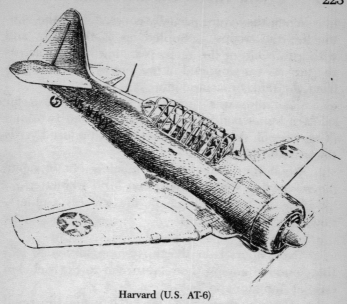

Harvard (U.S. AT-6)

"Christ!" Sloan muttered. "They're shooting at us!"

The Harvard flew frantically across the path of the tanks shaking its wings, through the thick of the crossfire which poured into the valley. At last, realizing their tragic error, the tank crews raced to meet the survivors and sheltered them behind their armoured hulls as they slowly reversed down the valley into safety.

The Squadron Commander directed the rescue from the open turret of his tank, shouting through his intercom. Blood streamed from an open wound in his head. Bullets rattled against the side of the tank like the mad beating of a drum.

When they were partially covered from the enemy fire the troops scrambled on to the tanks and withdrew. One of the men, swinging his foot across the turret, was wounded in the foot by a burst of fire from the tank's machine-gun.

Sloan also was injured. During the dash for safety a bullet had penetrated his leg, and two men of his platoon dragged him for the last hundred yards towards the tanks.

When they had withdrawn safely out of range Sloan asked if anybody had seen Mr Parkington.

A lance-corporal, one of the Vickers gunners, said, "He didn't make it."

A few hours later the thirty-nine survivors, less the wounded among them, returned to the Echelon base at Yongdungpo.

Here they were given food. They stood in small groups in the hastily improvised cookhouse, discussing their experiences, their nerves still too taut for sleep, and their eyes unnaturally bright from fatigue and disbelief.

On the day following their escape reinforcements began to arrive from the rear base in Kure.

Three days later the message went out from the battalion, "We are operational again."

XX

EPILOGUE

(December 20, 1951)

The trooper *Empire Fowey*, carrying the Gloucesters home from Korea in time for Christmas, slipped like a grey wraith through the mists gathering over Southampton Water. It was the end of a dull winter's day.

Hurst and Woodbridge, wearing the blue ribbon of the U.S. Presidential Citation on their shoulders, leaned over the rails of an upper deck and watched the oily wash lapping against the ship's sides. At intervals Hurst spat thoughtfully into the foam.

From a dockyard on shore the encroaching gloom was suddenly pierced by the glare of coloured lights and stars as a display of fireworks was touched off. Up and down the harbour sounded the doleful note of ships' sirens. A police launch escorting the ship in a trail of vaporous spray blew a succession of squeaks on its horn.

A trio of rusting tankers moored to a quayside raised such an excited trumpeting that the siren of one burst with a hiss of steam and a dying wail of protest.

Ahead loomed the massive dark bulk of the *Queen Elizabeth*.

"Wonder if she'll give us a toot?" Hurst said musingly.

As the *Empire Fowey* slowly drew level, the liner sent three deep and dignified blasts of her siren thundering through the dock area.

Both men were glad to be returning. Hurst looked forward avidly to the prospect of knotting together the loose ends of civil life; Woodbridge, who still had a few months of service to complete, simply wished to be home. Moreover, he would not be sorry to escape from the pent-up conditions of troopship life.

The rasping voice of the Tannoy system was to haunt him for months.

"Black discs to the cafeteria now!" it would snarl, or "The following personnel will report to the ship's orderly room—now!" There was no escaping it. It was diabolically impersonal. Woodbridge hated to think of himself as a unit of personnel, a black disc reporting to the cafeteria whenever the voice decreed.

The troop-decks, with their rows of three-tiered standees, one of which was his own for the voyage, depressed him. During the voyage through the prickly heat of the Red Sea, walking down the gangway at night to go to bed, he would not soon forget the reek of stale sweat, the concentrated odour of two hundred and fifty perspiring bodies which pervaded the whole troop-deck.

Now all this was over.

Very slowly the troopship drew in towards a brightly lit quay fronted by a balcony above the customs-sheds, packed with a cheering crowd, decorated with flags and bunting, noisy with gesticulating people.

Newsreel and television cameras began to operate. Reporters and cameramen stood in a tight cluster, waiting to board.

By a curious chance the Chinese had released the names of their prisoners on the previous day, and when the news-vendors came aboard Woodbridge looked at the placards and bought a paper.

Eagerly he ran through the list of the battalion's missing men who had been reported captured. Hurst followed the roll, looking over his shoulder.

"I notice Mr. Parkington is a prisoner," Woodbridge said.

"Laney isn't there," said Hurst.

"No."

There was a ruminative silence.

"They could easily have made mistakes," Woodbridge said at last.

Hurst stubbed out his cigarette and threw the butt overboard.

"Maybe."

The voice rasped through the Tannoy. "The following personnel will report to the head of the gangway—now!" A long list of names followed, including those of Woodbridge and Hurst.

"Willis is here," remarked Woodbridge, scanning the list.

"Anything about Powell?"

"Nothing."

"Will the following personnel please report to the head of the gangway," roared the voice, rising above the hubbub all over the ship. A shorter list of names followed.

"Pity about old Laney," Hurst said.

Woodbridge made no reply. He was thinking of an occasion months after the Imjin battle, when he had stood at the bottom of a hill near Solma-ri and watched the men of the U.S. Graves Commission bringing down bodies, each decorated with a cross, tied up in shapeless bundles of canvas. . . . They stared down over the towering sides of the ship with idle curiosity, watching the reunions taking place on the quay.

"I told my old Dutch not to bother," Hurst muttered. "Told 'er she'd be seein' more'n enough of me before long."

Woodbridge nodded, understanding.

"Will Corporal Woodbridge and Private Hurst," entreated the voice, "please report to the head of the gangway to meet their relatives."

"Why the bloody hell couldn't you say so before?" Hurst shouted towards the loudspeaker. At that moment Woodbridge was too overcome to speak.

They were home again.

The Gloucesters were home.